*He gazed into Sara's eyes and felt that elemental attraction again. So elemental, that he reminded himself he was here to talk to her.*

After Jase removed the banding around the bottle caps and used the corkscrew, he poured a sample of the first bottle of wine into two of the four juice glasses. "How long were you at the day-care center?"

"We finished around three."

He picked up one of the glasses and handed it to her. "I'm terrifically impressed with The Mommy Club. After I left there today, I had an idea about promoting it more, to get more people involved."

"What's your idea?" Sara's fingers brushed his when she took the glass. She was looking at him as if what he had to say was more important than taking a drink.

Damn, but he wanted to kiss her.

Dear Reader,

When our son was born, I was young, living in a new area and didn't have friends with newborns. Although my husband was a great dad and supportive in our new role, I was often nervous about it. But then I met another young mother and we took stroller walks with my son and her daughter. We talked and laughed, eventually carpooled and babysat for each other. That friendship and support meant so much.

The Mommy Club series is all about support, both emotional and practical, for families. In *Wanted: A Real Family,* Sara's house has burned to the ground. But Sara escaped with her most precious gift, her daughter. My hero, Jase Cramer, once Sara's patient in physical therapy, gives her a place to stay on beautiful Raintree Winery. A widow now, Sara admits her attraction to Jase and he can't deny his to her. Along with Jase's moral support, she receives the friendship she needs from the women of The Mommy Club. Sara's friends will have their own books in the upcoming months.

I hope you enjoy this series. May you always have love and friendship in your life.

Karen Rose Smith

# Wanted: A Real Family

—

## Karen Rose Smith

HARLEQUIN® SPECIAL EDITION®

Recycling programs
for this product may
not exist in your area.

ISBN-13: 978-0-373-65759-9

WANTED: A REAL FAMILY

**Printed in U.S.A.**

## Books by Karen Rose Smith

### Harlequin Special Edition

¤*His Country Cinderella* #2137
**\*\****Once Upon a Groom* #2146
**\*\****The CEO's Unexpected Proposal* #2201
**\*\****Riley's Baby Boy* #2205
¶*Wanted: A Real Family* #2277

### Silhouette Special Edition

*Abigail and Mistletoe* #930
*The Sheriff's Proposal* #1074
*His Little Girl's Laughter* #1426
*Expecting the CEO's Baby* #1535
*Their Baby Bond* #1588
*Take a Chance on Me* #1599
*Which Child Is Mine?* #1655
Δ*Cabin Fever* #1682
Ω*Custody for Two* #1753
Ω*The Baby Trail* #1767
Ω*Expecting His Brother's Baby* #1779
+*The Super Mom* #1797
§*Falling for the Texas Tycoon* #1807
±*The Daddy Dilemma* #1884
^*Her Mr. Right?* #1897
±*The Daddy Plan* #1908
±*The Daddy Verdict* #1925
\**Lullaby for Two* #1961
\**The Midwife's Glass Slipper* #1972
Φ*The Texas Bodyguard's Proposal* #1987
\**Baby by Surprise* #1997
\**The Texas Billionaire's Baby* #2032
\**The Texan's Happily-Ever-After* #2044
Ψ*From Doctor...to Daddy* #2065
\**Twins Under His Tree* #2087
**\*\****His Daughter...Their Child* #2098

### Silhouette Books

The Fortunes of Texas
*Marry in Haste...*

Logan's Legacy
*A Precious Gift*

The Fortunes of Texas: Reunion
*The Good Doctor*

Signature Select

*Secret Admirer*
"Dream Marriage"

ΩBaby Bonds
ΔMontana Mavericks:
     Gold Rush Grooms
+Talk of the Neighborhood
§Logan's Legacy Revisited
^The Wilder Family
±Dads in Progress
 \*The Baby Experts
ΦThe Foleys and the McCords
ΨMontana Mavericks:
     Thunder Canyon Cowboys
**Reunion Brides
¤Montana Mavericks:
     The Texans are Coming!
¶The Mommy Club

Other titles by this author
available in ebook format.

---

## KAREN ROSE SMITH

Award-winning and bestselling author Karen Rose Smith began writing in her early teens. An only child, she spent a lot of time in her imagination and with books—Nancy Drew, Zane Grey, the Black Stallion and Anne of Green Gables. Her plotlines include small communities and family relationships as part of everyday living. Residing in Pennsylvania with her husband and three cats, she welcomes interaction with readers on Facebook, Twitter @karenrosesmith and through email at her website, www.karenrosesmith.com, where they can sign up for her newsletter.

To Heather,
a good friend and one of the best mommies I know.

## *Chapter One*

Sara Stevens took her eyes from the long driveway nestled between rows and rows of grape trellises, colorful rose gardens and mountains in the distance. Glancing over her shoulder into the back where her four-year-old daughter sat in her car seat, she noticed Amy was staring out the window. Amy was as shaken as she was. She could tell when her little girl was quiet any length of time. She'd been quiet since Sara had awakened her a few nights ago in a house filled with smoke and carried her to safety.

Had that only been a few nights ago?

They'd lost everything they'd possessed, except their car. The loss weighed heavily on Sara. But right now, what weighed on her most was the decision she'd have to make regarding their living arrangements. Going through the channels of The Mommy Club, an organization in Fawn Grove, California, that helped parents in need, Jase Cramer had invited her and Amy to stay in the guesthouse at the nearby Raintree Winery.

But she and Jase had a history. She was just coming to look at the guesthouse today. Maybe she could find another place to stay.

Or maybe not.

As she drove up to the gravel parking area at the guest cottage, she spotted Jase standing by the door in the mid-May sun. His wavy black hair was shaggy, his gray eyes still intense. Craggy lines had etched his face, no doubt from the sights he'd witnessed in his former career. His physical therapy had ended two years ago. What had happened to him since?

She was about to find out.

He was so tall and muscular, now tanned from his work on the vineyard rather than his former profession as a photographer and journalist who told the rest of the world about children in refugee camps.

She shouldn't be so unsettled about this meeting. She was a widow now, after all. But seeing him again took her back two years to a time when her life had been different, to a time when she'd thought she'd been happy, to a time before her marriage had been rocked and her world as she'd known it had blown up.

She opened her car door, and he offered her his hand. "Sara. It's good to see you again. I'm just sorry it's under these circumstances."

His voice was still that deep warm baritone that seemed to vibrate through her. "How did you know about the fire?"

"I saw your interview on the news."

Sara nodded. "Right after the fire. That reporter wouldn't stop asking questions."

"You *were* the news. You saved your daughter from a burning house. That's heroic."

"Not heroic. I couldn't have left her. She's my heart."

After studying her for several long moments, Jase peered into the backseat. "How is she doing?"

"She doesn't understand what happened. Kaitlyn Foster has made us feel at home in her guest room, but Amy is confused by it all."

"Why don't we take a look at the guesthouse? Maybe she'll like the cottage and the vineyard."

A few minutes later, Sara held Amy's hand as they stepped over the threshold of Raintree Winery's guesthouse.

"What do you think?" Jase asked, motioning to the exposed beams, the empty living room with a native stone fireplace and kitchen and dining area beyond. The golden polished flooring, the rough plastered walls and the birch cabinets she could glimpse in the kitchen added lightness to the space already glowing with sunlight from the windows.

Amy burrowed into her mother's side and Sara crouched down, hanging her arm around her daughter's shoulders. "Isn't this pretty?"

Amy just poked her finger into her mouth and looked down at her sneakers.

Jase crouched down with Sara. "You can have your own bedroom here. There are two, one for your mom and one for you. And, if you're lucky, you might even catch sight of a deer outside your window. Or a hummingbird. Have you ever seen a hummingbird? They're tiny and flap their wings really fast."

Sara could see Jase had caught Amy's attention now, and her daughter actually gazed over at him.

"They like to flit around the columbine."

"Can I catch a hummingbird?" Amy asked.

"Probably not. But if we hang a feeder on the porch, you might see them more often."

Sara rose to her feet, the idea of catching a glimpse of a hummingbird entrancing her, too.

After another smile for Amy, Jase also rose. "Kaitlyn told me furniture won't be a problem. Apparently The Mommy Club has storage sheds full of stuff for emergencies like this, as well as people donating."

With a sigh, Sara closed her eyes.

Jase stepped a little closer. "What's wrong?"

"I don't want to accept all this help. I don't want to be a charity case."

"Sara," he said with so much gentleness, tears almost came to her eyes. "This is temporary. Living here and accepting help is temporary. Didn't you once tell me I had to get over my pride and rethink my life to make it work again?"

The fact that he remembered her words from when she'd been his physical therapist touched her. He'd been at an emotional as well as a physical low, not ready to give up the life he'd wanted to pursue. While photographing children outside a refugee camp in Kenya, he and a few other aid workers had been injured by a marauding band of criminals. For some reason, the last thing he'd wanted to do was return to his father and Raintree Winery and make a place for himself here. She'd never known the real reason why, but she *had* known other details about Jase's life, details that now made her wonder if everyone experienced betrayal at one point or another. His fiancée had been unfaithful.

"Your memory is too good," she murmured, wondering what else he remembered about what she'd told him while he was in treatment with her.

He chuckled. "I only remember the important stuff."

He cast a glance down at Amy. "Don't you think she'd be happy here? Plenty of room to wander. For you, too. I hear long walks are therapeutic."

This time Sara had to laugh, and it was almost a strange sensation for her. Her life had been nothing but serious the past couple of years. "Did you follow all the advice I gave you?"

"Not all, but most. I wanted to get well…and strong."

He was obviously strong again. Although he wore jeans and a white oxford shirt with the sleeves rolled up, she could see the muscles underneath when he moved. After all, as a physical therapist, she quickly assessed the condition of muscles. He'd been way too lean when she'd treated him. Now he'd built up muscle all over. From the looks of his flat stomach, he had strength there, too.

Jase Cramer wasn't handsome in the usual sense. Those lines around his eyes and along his mouth were a little deeper than they should be at his thirty-six years. But there was an intensity about Jase, a deep passion that hadn't been so evident when he'd first come to her as a patient, but had been revitalized by the end of his therapy.

"Let's take a look at the bedrooms," he suggested.

*Empty bedrooms,* she reminded herself, feeling an unexpected spark deep down inside whenever her gaze met his. *Not going to happen,* she warned herself. If she and Amy did accept Jase's kind offer, they would only stay as long as it took for her to get back on her financial feet.

One bedroom was smaller than the other, but both were adequate, and there was one bathroom they'd share. It was a cozy guesthouse and she wondered why it was empty.

"Do you rent this out?"

"My father hasn't done that since before I returned home. While I was growing up, our housekeeper lived here, but he let her go when I went to college. Friends have stayed here on and off for vacations, that kind of thing, before my father emptied it. He updated it by refinishing the floors and putting in new appliances. He likes everything to be in tip-top shape, even if he doesn't use it."

Sara had noticed Jase rarely referred to his father as his dad. That seemed kind of odd but she'd never questioned him about it.

"Your father's okay with us staying here?"

Jase frowned. "I'll be honest with you. He doesn't like a lot of people around. Our chief winemaker, Liam Corbett, has an apartment above the winery and he's used to him living there. So he had reservations about inviting you here. But he couldn't give me a good reason not to. I promised him you wouldn't have wild parties that lasted all weekend."

Again, she had to smile. "No wild parties," she assured him.

When they returned to the living room, Jase dropped down into a crouch again to be on eye level with Amy. "I didn't ask your mom first," he said with a wink. "You can make the decision for both of you. How would you like a sweet treat? I have sweet rolls made with grape jelly from vineyard grapes. They'd be great with a glass of milk for a late breakfast."

Amy looked up at her mom with pleading eyes. She loved sweets and Sara usually limited them to cookies as a bedtime snack. But Amy had been through so much, she didn't have the heart to deny her a treat. She had lost her toys in the fire. She'd slept with Sara the past few nights in Kaitlyn's spare room. She'd asked Sara when they were going home, and it had been so hard to explain to a four-year-old that they didn't have a home anymore.

Jase rose to his feet, and when Sara gazed into his eyes, she said, "I think a sweet treat is just what we all need."

As they walked toward the main house, Sara looked out over the vineyard. It was an absolutely beautiful setting. Jase had once told her it encompassed over two hundred acres. Clover covered some fields. Lush green was everywhere, from the trees and shrubs, to the trellises of grapevines. There were deep, rich scents here, from the earthy damp ground to the roses. It was crazy, but she almost felt like a different person here. Maybe she and Amy had made a mistake by staying in the house that Conrad had bought them to the detriment of them all. When she'd married Conrad, she'd loved him in a naive, too-trusting way. Over the course of her marriage, she'd explicitly learned how one-sided trust could destroy everything.

Although she was close by Sara's side, Amy nevertheless seemed eager to follow Jase. She was used to other kids being around her in day care, but as for adults, mostly women were in and out of her life. In the past year, Sara hadn't thought about it much, but male role models were important to little girls, too.

Stone steps led to the polished walnut back door of the main house. Jase opened it and they stepped inside a cavernous kitchen. This room held none of the warmth of the cottage, though it did have a brick fireplace with a rounded arch and fire screen. The appliances were shiny stainless steel and they looked as if they, too, had been replaced recently. The granite counters gleamed and the copper pots hanging from the ceiling above the sink looked as if they'd never been used. There weren't any colorful place mats on the oak pedestal table, or flowered curtains at the windows. The blinds were tilted closed, not letting in much light.

Jase pointed to the counter and the glass-domed dish. The sweet rolls were a confectioner's delight and Amy's eyes grew wide along with her smile.

"Can I, Mommy?"

"Sure, you can. But I think we'll need plenty of napkins to go along with the sweet roll."

Jase pulled dishes from a cupboard and a few napkins from another. They all sat at the table. Amy was happily biting into jelly, sweet icing and pastry when Jase said, "In your interview, I heard you lost your husband a year ago. I'm sorry."

Sara tore off a piece of a roll but suddenly had no appetite for it. Thanks to real-time research, the journalist who'd interviewed her had already known much of her background. "Yes, it was a year ago."

"Was it sudden?" Jase prompted.

"A heart attack."

Jase's expression turned questioning, so she added, "He was fifteen years older than I was. Forty-four. The doctor said whatever triggered it might have been a congenital abnormality."

And physically, she knew that was certainly true. But the stress in his life definitely hadn't helped. She tried to keep herself from feeling guilty, but she was to blame, too—for being so blind. She hadn't known he'd taken on a supersized mortgage. She hadn't known about his credit card debt. As a new wife, first pregnant and then busy with an infant as well as work, she'd let Conrad handle their finances. She hadn't asked enough questions. She'd trusted too much.

Jase's eyes were kind as he looked at her, and her heart started thumping faster as she thought she saw more than kindness there.

Unexpectedly, Amy laid very sticky fingers on Jase's shirtsleeve and asked, "Can I have some milk?"

"Oh, Amy." Grape jelly streaked the white fabric of Jase's shirt. Over the years, Sara had found men didn't like the messiness of kids. Conrad had never wanted to feed Amy himself when she was a baby, so it was automatic for Sara to jump up, grab a napkin and try to fix the mess. Had she resented that he didn't seem to love their daughter as much as she did?

She dabbed at Jase's sleeve, smearing the jelly more. Her fingers slipped from the material to his arm. His skin was hot, his hair rough, and when she met his gaze—

The inordinate silence when their awareness of each other took hold was enough to rattle her bones.

"Mommy, I'm sorry," Amy wailed.

Sara knew she was making a mess of this whole thing. She wrapped her arm around her daughter. "It's okay. We'll wash Mr. Cramer's shirt. We'll fix this."

Jase clasped her shoulder. "It's okay. Relax. It's just a shirt."

He addressed Amy. "Sticky fingers and sweet rolls go together. Let me get that milk." He rolled both of his sleeves up further to cover the jelly and grinned at Amy. "See? All fixed."

He motioned for Sara to sit again. "You're too jumpy. You need to take a walk through the vineyard and relax." Then he must have realized he'd chided her and shook his head. "Sorry. I have no right to give you advice. I can't imagine what losing your home was like."

Then, to Sara's astonishment, Jase went to the sink, ripped a paper towel from the roll under the counter, wet it and sat down with Amy. "Here, let's get some of that jelly off. Your milk will slide through your fingers."

"I'll do that." Sara reached for the towel in his hand. With instant clarity, she remembered some of the photos in the paper and online of Jase feeding little children who were malnourished, of him holding one Amy's age in his arms.

His fingers covered hers as she took the towel. "You've

got to relax," he said again. "Everything is going to get better."

His touch sent tingles through her. That was odd. After all, she'd treated him…she'd touched him when he was her patient. But as with all patients, she'd closed herself off against any personal feelings. She'd been married and she'd ignored vibrations coming from men who were anything more than just friendly. But now, today, it was like the floodgates had opened. Everything about Jase Cramer made her feel overly sensitized to him.

Sara had torn off a piece of her sweet roll and tasted it when Jase brought three tall glasses of milk to the table. Amy's was only half-full, and again Sara appreciated his knowledge of kids.

Sara was watching Amy drink from the tall glass without spilling it when she heard footsteps outside the kitchen doorway.

Ethan Cramer entered the room. She recognized him from photos in the paper about him and Raintree Winery. Raintree Wines had won awards and Fawn Grove lauded their citizens who made good.

Having never met Ethan Cramer, Sara didn't know what to expect, but she was sensitive to his expression of disapproval as his gaze fell on her and Amy. Jase and his father looked nothing alike.

Where Jase was all dark intensity, black hair and gray eyes, his father's hair was blond and thinning. His blue eyes were sharp as he asked his son, "This is Ms. Stevens?"

"Yes, this is Sara and her daughter."

"I'm sorry you lost your home," Ethan said while studying her.

She didn't know quite what to say to that. She didn't know what was behind his words, but something was. Jase had told her his father was on board if she and Amy wanted to stay in the cottage, but now she wondered if that was really true.

"Jase invited us over for some sweet rolls while I decide if we want to stay in the cottage or not. It's very kind of you to offer it."

"Jase offered it, and I agreed it was the right thing to do. But as soon as you're back on your feet, I expect you'll find your own place again."

"Father!"

"Mr. Cramer, if you'd rather we not use the cottage, I will find somewhere else."

Jase, who had been looking more tense and even more frustrated, stepped in. "If it weren't for Sara, I wouldn't have recovered as fast as I did to help you here. I owe her a debt of gratitude."

"Yes, I know you do," Ethan said with a sigh, just looking weary now. "And when her stay here is over, we'll consider your debt repaid." Ethan focused on Sara. "Have you made a decision?"

Their circumstances seemed less than ideal, yet her options were limited as were her finances. She was fairly certain she and Amy could stay out of Ethan Cramer's way. Amy would be at day care during the week and Sara would be working. In the evening, they could easily keep to themselves. Weekends they would be busy with errands and rebuilding their life. They had no reason to run into Ethan Cramer, or even Jase, for that matter. Sunshine, space to wander and a room of her own would be good for Amy. Sara would be foolish not to accept.

"Raintree Winery is a beautiful place. Amy needs a little bit of that right now until we can start sewing our lives back together. So we'd like to stay in the cottage for a while."

Ethan gave a nod, then addressed Jase. "Don't forget,

you're supposed to meet with Liam and me over at the winery at one. I want to discuss the new barrels."

"I won't forget."

Jase's voice was tight and Sara wondered if the tension she sensed between father and son was just about her and Amy staying here or if it went further back than that. Had Ethan wanted Jase to work here all along while Jase had wanted to photograph the world and wander? But now that Jase was back, didn't Ethan Cramer have what he wanted?

With a nod, Ethan left the kitchen and closed the door behind him.

Amy had seemed unaware of the undercurrent. She was finishing her sweet roll with swigs of milk every once in a while, getting sticky icing all over her mouth and fingers again.

Sara crossed the room to the sink for another wet paper towel. Jase followed her and stood beside her.

"I don't know what got into him," Jase said.

"Is he usually so…frosty?"

"He's always been remote and sometimes cold. I've accepted that."

"I don't understand."

"Ethan Cramer isn't my father. He's my adoptive father."

"I didn't know that."

"I don't talk about it. The people who have lived in Fawn Grove all their lives know."

"I moved here after I earned my master's in PT."

"Where did you grow up?"

"San Francisco. I went to college at Berkeley."

"Is your family still there?"

"I lost my parents the day I graduated from college. They were in an accident on the way there."

"Sara." He put his hands on her shoulders and turned her toward him. "You've known too much loss."

"Everyone has losses. Everyone misses their loved ones. I think, though, the missing's always there and we have to figure out a way to put it in perspective. I did that by focusing on getting my master's and helping wherever I could in my practice. But I needed a fresh start, so I went to a placement professional. She found me the position in Fawn Grove. I've been happy here."

"Until this past year."

Until before that, really, but Jase didn't know that. His hands on her shoulders felt as if they belonged there. His close proximity led her to study his high cheekbones, his cleft chin, the scars along one temple that were white against his tan.

Suddenly Jase released her and leaned away. She saw something in his eyes and wondered if it had to do with his relationships with women…with the fiancée who'd deserted him when he was at his lowest.

For whatever reason, she was glad he'd backed away. She wasn't about to get involved with any man again, not even one who seemed to have a rapport with kids, not even one whose mere looks could cause a zing up her nerve endings. Not involved. Never again. Not ever.

## Chapter Two

After his shower, Jase paced his suite in the main house Saturday morning. Sara would be here soon, as well as The Mommy Club volunteers. He just hoped his decision to invite Sara and her daughter to Raintree hadn't been a mistake.

The only mistake he'd made up to this point in his life had been getting involved with Dana. She'd been tempting, exciting and energized with enthusiasm for her career. He hadn't seen beyond the curves and sex appeal. He'd begun dreaming of a life they could share. But Dana had latched on to another man as if he'd been a lifeline away from Jase, what had happened to him, his injuries and an uncertain recovery. She'd bailed in the most damaging of ways and Jase still stung from her betrayal and her attitude about it.

For the past two years, Jase had poured every waking moment into making Raintree the most successful vineyard in California. There had been no time for women or their machinations.

He grabbed a pair of clean jeans from the closet and dressed. The problem was—he didn't categorize Sara with other women. Because of her, he had full use of his shoulder. Because of her, his strength had slowly returned, his muscle tone had increased and his attitude about his life had done a one-eighty.

Honesty made him admit he'd been attracted to her when he'd been her patient, but he'd seen that ring on her finger. He'd heard her tenderly talk about her two-year-old daughter. He would have never messed with that.

The devil on his shoulder seemed to whisper, *She's a widow now.*

Maybe so. But she was a homeless, vulnerable widow and he'd never take advantage of that. Besides, he'd given up on white picket fences and vows that lasted forever. Nothing good lasted forever—not in his experience. And the truth of it was he didn't believe he could ever trust a woman again.

Had he made the right decision asking Sara to Raintree? His father was on edge. And Jase himself wasn't sure how this situation would play out.

It was temporary. It would play out…and life as he'd come to know it would go on.

*Grateful* didn't even begin to describe how Sara felt as Jase helped one of The Mommy Club volunteers carry a sofa in a pretty mauve-and-green-flowered slipcover into the cottage. This was moving day. She still didn't know if she'd made the right decision coming to Raintree Winery, but watching Amy coloring under a live oak, the sun-dappled blanket around her, she was surer today than she had been for the past week.

Jase stood in the doorway and beckoned to her. He hadn't even broken a sweat. His broad shoulders filled the space and she couldn't see behind him. He'd been careful this morning not to get too close. She'd been careful about proximity, too.

When Sara glanced toward Amy, Jase assured her, "She's fine. She knows exactly where you are." He motioned to his assistant, Marissa, who was dropping another pack of markers beside Amy. "Will you keep an eye on her?" he called.

Marissa smiled and nodded.

"Marissa's the one who knew all about The Mommy Club and gave me Kaitlyn's number. Apparently the organization helped her when she was pregnant."

Then, glancing inside the cottage, he changed the subject back to the situation at hand. "You need to tell us which wall would be the best backing for the sofa."

Sara hadn't seen Jase since the day she'd visited Raintree to decide about the cottage. She'd spoken to him on the phone a few times to make arrangements for today, and each time, the sound of his voice had lingered long after the call.

She glanced up at the hummingbird feeder he'd hung on the porch and had to smile. When he stood aside to let her enter, she was aware of his aftershave and trying not to be.

The sofa sat crosswise in the living room. Her attention was focused more on Jase than on the furniture. Still, she eyed the space instead of his gray eyes.

"Let's not put it against a wall," she said. "Let's move it in front of the fireplace. Amy and I can curl up there on cool nights. We can put that wing chair by the window and Amy can watch TV from there."

"Don't *you* watch TV?"

"Not so much. If I do settle down on the sofa at night

after Amy goes to bed, I usually conk out." Or she sat in the silence and worried about how she was going to pay the bills. But Jase didn't need to know that. If she confided in him about Conrad and about the debts, she'd be opening the door to confidences she didn't know she was ready to share…didn't know if she'd ever be ready for again.

Steering the subject away from her personal life, Sara commented, "I wonder where all this furniture came from. If it was used, it's been repainted and repaired like new."

"I did a little digging and found out there are a lot of guardian angels in The Mommy Club, from someone depositing funds in a never-ending account, to all the volunteers who lend a helping hand."

Kaitlyn Foster slipped into the small cottage. She was a striking woman, with blond hair and green eyes, who could make any woman envious of her. But her personality as a compassionate pediatrician was as striking as her good looks. That compassion seemed to extend to all areas of her life. She'd been so kind to Sara after the fire and so good with Amy.

Now she was carrying a small bedside lamp in pink and white, perfect for a little girl's room. "I just have to plug this in and Amy's room is ready. The sheets are on the bed if you want to make it."

"I don't know how I'm ever going to repay The Mommy Club. Is there anything I can do to help kids or a family who needs it?"

Kaitlyn said, "We have a food drive coming up, as well as a summer program for kids and parents. We provide lunches and food baskets for families who are down on their luck and kids who are hungry. All of it makes a difference. Even if lunch is just a sandwich with an apple, the kids act like it's a gourmet meal. We can always use help. After you get settled in, we can talk about it more."

Jase suddenly said, "I'd like to help, too."

Both women stared at him.

"What? A man can't help The Mommy Club? I can donate funds and a little time. Sure, I'm as busy as the next guy, but helping kids—that used to be my life's goal."

Again some of the pictures Jase had taken and stories he'd written ran through Sara's mind. She knew precisely what had happened to change his life's goal. What exactly was his goal now? Did he miss his old life?

After Kaitlyn said again she'd be in touch about the food drive and headed toward Amy's room, Jase moved away from Sara, took one end of the sofa and pushed it where she wanted it in front of the fireplace. "How's that?"

"Perfect. If you ever tire of making wine, you can move furniture," she joked.

He gazed straight out the window to the winery. When his gaze met hers again, she thought she saw a bit of longing in his eyes. Just what did Jase Cramer long for?

He studied her and then came closer, his voice low and a bit husky. He said, "The only reason I can push that sofa around is the physical therapy you gave me."

"Jase—"

"Don't tell me it isn't so."

"Any therapist who took you on as a patient could have strengthened your arm and shoulder and put you on an exercise regimen to make you healthy again."

"I don't know if I believe that. It was your caring and your positive outlook that made me see I could have a future here, that photojournalism wasn't the be-all and end-all. You provided more than physical therapy, Sara. I imagine you do with all your patients."

She felt herself blushing, a condition she'd had since childhood that affected her when she was nervous or upset. Now she was neither of them, but she was blushing anyway.

As she looked into Jase's face and saw he really meant what he said, her heart raced. At the V-neck of his T-shirt, black hair curled against his tan skin. She remembered the scars on his shoulder, the line across his stomach where bullets had almost been the death of him. A field doctor at the refugee camp had done emergency surgery and saved his life under awful conditions. Yes, Jase was lucky to be alive. She knew what the experience had cost him—the notes were in his medical records.

Amy suddenly came running in and wrapped her arms around Sara's legs. It was a relief to take her attention away from Jase and give it to her daughter. Her first and foremost concern always had to be Amy. "What's up, Bitsy Bug?"

"I'm not a bitsy bug. I'm Amy."

Sara hugged her daughter. "Did you get lonely out there?"

"I want to see my room."

"We can do that. It's not completely ready yet. Maybe you can help me make the bed."

"Can Mr. Jase help, too?" Amy looked up at Jase with a wide smile, obviously accepting him into her world. That sweet roll had gone a long way, but his attitude had, too. He didn't just tolerate Amy, he conversed with her. He got down on her level. A kid could smell a phony a mile away and Jase was no phony.

"I'm sure Mr. Cramer has so many more things to do than help make your bed."

Jase shrugged. "I took the morning to help. Let's go see what your room looks like." He held out his hand to Amy.

Her daughter didn't hesitate to take it. Jase was so tall, and Amy, so small. Living on the Raintree Winery property, just how often would they see him?

There was a single bed in Amy's room with a white

wood headboard. The short dresser had a child-sized mirror hanging above it. Beside the bed, someone had unfolded a latch-hook rug with adorable kittens scampering on it. A sealed package of new pink sheets, a soft pink blanket and a pink-and-white gingham spread with ruffles lay at the foot of the bed.

"I like pink," Amy said as if wondering why her mother was hesitating. The truth was, Sara's throat felt thick and her chest a little tight. Someone had done this for her daughter and she was so thankful for that.

Without her saying a word, Jase seemed to understand. He unfolded the spread and laid it over the wooden rocking chair by the side of the bed. Patting the mattress, he said to Amy, "Try it out. See what you think. You shouldn't jump on it, but you can bounce a little."

Forgetting her mom for the moment, Amy crawled up onto the bed and bounced up and down. "It's soft."

Jase had already ripped open the package of sheets. He flipped the pillowcase to Amy. "See if you can put the pillow in that. It will be a big help."

After Amy jumped off the bed, Sara helped her daughter stuff the pillow into the fabric. By then, Jase had the bottom sheet spread on the bed and tucked in.

"Do this often?" Sara teased.

But he said casually, "I'm used to setting up camp. This isn't all that different. It's sort of like riding a bike. You never forget how."

"When you were a kid and living here, I bet you didn't have to make your own bed."

A shadow crossed Jase's face. She'd seen those shadows before when he was remembering something he didn't want to remember. She could understand that with regard to his injuries and his broken engagement, but with regard to his childhood?

"The housekeeper took care of that."

"Does your father have help with the house now?" Certainly, he must.

"We have a cook who comes in three times a week. She prepares food and makes sure the refrigerator's stocked. A cleaning lady also comes in once a week. As I said, my father didn't particularly like someone else around all the time."

"But he agreed to let me stay here because it's temporary."

"Something like that."

She laid the pillow on the bed, then lightly touched his forearm. "Because you convinced him."

"I don't want you to worry about what my father thinks."

"But I do."

"My father dislikes any change, so don't take his attitude personally. He's used to Liam coming and going over the winery. He'll get used to you and Amy, too. He's a solitary man, Sara. He has a couple of close friends but everyone else is a business contact."

She wondered what Jase was trying to tell her, but Amy was tugging on her arm and she knew her daughter would soon be needing lunch.

"Can I have some juice? I'm thirsty."

"I think I saw some boxes of apple juice in one of the bags. How about one of them?" Jase asked. "Come on, let's go get one while your mom finishes the bed."

Whatever Jase had been trying to tell her, the moment was gone now. If she knew more about Ethan Cramer, maybe she and Amy wouldn't have to tiptoe around him.

As Jase and Amy left the room and Sara picked up the spread, she realized she wanted to know more about *Jase*. But curiosity could get her into deep trouble.

\* \* \*

Jase stepped out of the storage shed beside the winery the next day, toolbox in one hand, a toy store bag in the other. Earlier, he had seen Sara leave with Amy and guessed she was going to church first thing on a Sunday morning. She'd returned a little while ago and he had some repairs to make on the cottage, a few details he hadn't noticed before she'd moved in.

He should stay away from her…he really should. Her husband had only been gone a year and she was vulnerable now, after losing her home. But there was something about Sara that made him want to be around her. Chemistry? Sure, that was part of it. He wasn't in denial. She turned him on. A woman hadn't done that in a long time. But there was something else, too. Something to do with the way she looked at the world.

Still, he was going to keep his distance. That was best for both of them. When he knocked on the door to the cottage and Sara opened it, she looked surprised. "Jase, hi. We just got back from church and changed clothes."

Uh-huh, he'd been right. She'd changed into a flowered blouse and yellow shorts that complemented it. She'd braided her hair at both temples and looked more like a teenager than a thirty-year-old physical therapist.

"I hope I'm not interrupting anything. Yesterday I noticed the screen door is off center a bit and the windows in the bedroom won't open without a lot of effort. Do you mind if I fix them while I have the time?"

"No, I don't mind. I did have trouble opening Amy's window this morning. Come on in. We're still trying to make it our own." She pointed to Amy who was coloring on the coffee table. "She's drawing some pictures to hang in her room. If that's okay. I can get those sticky things for the walls so I don't make holes."

"Make all the holes you want. They can be patched." He glanced at the bag in his other hand, leaned close to Sara and said in a low voice, "I have something for Amy. I know she lost most of her toys. Do you mind if I give it to her?"

"You didn't have to do that."

"I know, but I want to. I bought it last week after I knew you were going to move in."

There was something close to admiration in Sara's eyes, and he was surprised how that filled him with a sense of satisfaction.

"Can you come here a minute?" Sara called to her daughter.

Amy looked up, saw Jase and smiled shyly.

"I found a friend for you," he said to her. "He barked at me when I passed him in the store."

Amy's eyes widened. "He did?"

Most kids were innocent. They could believe so easily. "Reach into the bag and see if he'll come out and play."

Amy checked with Sara. "Can I?"

"Go ahead."

Amy reached into the bag and drew out a mop of a stuffed dog with black-and-white fur that fell down into his eyes.

"Do you like him?" Jase asked.

"Is he mine?"

"He can be if you name him."

"He looks like Mom's mop. Can I name him Moppy?"

"That works for me. I bet he can help you color."

Amy ran over to the coffee table once more and set him there, right on her drawing. But Sara called her back. "What do you say to Mr. Jase?"

Amy glanced at him and smiled. "Thank you."

"You're most welcome."

"I doubt if she'll go anywhere without him. Someone

donated a doll with a baby carriage, but she does love stuffed toys." Sara came a little closer to him and whispered, "She lost her favorite in the fire—a teddy bear."

Sara was close enough to touch, almost close enough to kiss. Absolutely crazy thought. That's not why he was here. That's definitely not why he'd asked her to stay. He had a debt to repay to her for giving him back his life. But she smelled so damn good, too. When he'd seen her for physical therapy, he'd figured out she must use some kind of strawberry shampoo or conditioner on her hair because it was her hair that smelled so good.

Backing away, he said, "I don't want to interrupt whatever you were doing. I'll work on Amy's bedroom window first." He picked up his toolbox and went to the smaller of the two bedrooms, unable to shake the image of him running his fingers through Sara's hair.

Ten minutes later, Jase had finished with the windows in the two bedrooms. He noticed Sara sitting at the kitchen table, several sheaves of paper in front of her. But he didn't ask what they were. They were none of his business.

"I'm going to have to take the screen door off its hinges and plane the bottom section. The wood just warped. I could have an aluminum door put on if you'd rather have that."

"I like the wooden one. I like the old-fashioned look of it. That's what's so welcoming about this cottage, the fact that it's not a cookie-cutter image of all others."

"I suppose you like the ivy, too? Dad's been wanting the gardener to tear it all down for a while. They always have an argument about it."

"I like the ivy, too." She began mounding the papers and inserting them into an accordion file.

When his gaze fell on it, she explained, "This file of documents and receipts was in my car so it survived the fire. I was going to make copies. It's ironic I was having trouble with my garage door opener so my car was parked in front of the house. Otherwise, that might have gone up in flames, too."

"I guess that's what optimists call a silver lining." He went to the screen door and began loosening the hinges.

"I was just about to make lunch. Along with the clothes and furniture the volunteers brought, they stocked my refrigerator and freezer. Do you like stir-fry? You're welcome to stay, unless you and your dad eat Sunday dinner together."

Jase hesitated before answering and Sara took that the wrong way. Her face flushed a little. "It's okay if you'd rather not."

Glancing at Amy, seeing she was lost in what she was doing and not paying any attention to them, he said, "Most of the folks in Fawn Grove who have lived here all of their lives know my history with Raintree Winery."

"Your history?" Plainly, Sara didn't understand.

He didn't confide in many people. He didn't relive what he'd rather forget. That was true for childhood as well as some of his photojournalistic experiences. But Sara was living here and she might as well know the truth. It might make her feel better about Ethan's attitude.

"As I mentioned, Ethan Cramer's not my biological father. I was twelve and in the foster care system when he adopted me."

Sara was looking up at him now, her golden-brown eyes compassionate, her attitude completely attentive.

Her understanding gaze and silent concentration on him urged him to go on. "My father and I have never been that…close. Maybe I was too old when I came to live here. Maybe he was too set in his ways. We've never really talked about it. But we also never had a normal father-son bond."

"Is that the reason when you came back here two years ago that you didn't know if you could find a life here?"

"That was a big part of it. The vineyard itself I'd always been drawn to. I started working with the grapes soon after I arrived. My father would show me what to do and I'd do it. Pruning and tying the vines weren't just chores, because the whole process fascinated me. I learned quickly and easily about the varieties of grapes, the soil, the process of wine-making. My father and I found common ground with what he did here. But other than that— I don't know if I was completely closed off or if he was. Maybe taking on a twelve-year-old was more than he bargained for. But anyway, since I've been back, except for the vineyard, we've had separate lives."

"That's a shame," Sara said. "You're living here together. You should be able to retrace some steps and find understanding."

"Maybe that's what neither of us wants."

"But you should."

"Sara," he said with a warning note in his voice.

"Jase, I have no family, except for Amy. Do you think for a minute I'd ever let anything come between us?"

"You're a good mom, Sara. Of course you believe that. But I wasn't an innocent kid with no baggage when I arrived here." He saw the questions in her eyes, but he wasn't going to answer them.

"No matter what baggage you had, every child just wants to be loved. Heck, every adult just wants to be loved."

When she said the words, she looked a bit embarrassed. Was she looking for love again? "You'd get married again?"

"Oh, no."

The way she said it, Jase had a feeling her marriage hadn't been everything she'd wanted it to be. "Do you want to elaborate a bit?"

"Not really."

Of course she didn't. He was treading into private territory and he knew it. "Want to rescind your offer of dinner?"

She looked tempted but shook her head. "No, we'll just make a pact not to discuss anything too…personal."

They'd already discussed some things that were personal when he was in physical therapy. After all, Dana's infidelity had been a huge part of his pessimistic attitude when he'd returned home. "I'd like to stay. It will be a nice break before I head back to the office for the afternoon."

"Working on a Sunday?"

"A vineyard is similar to a farm. Anything that grows doesn't take a vacation, and neither does the work that piles up because of it. I have a meeting with Liam later to go over a new organic process. Have you met him yet?"

"No, I haven't."

"He's a friendly guy, sometimes too friendly with the ladies. He dates someone new every weekend."

"How old is he?"

"Older than I am—forty-five."

"And you're thirty-six."

"You remember?"

"Therapists never forget some of their patients."

Her words made his heart thump louder and that was silly. She could just mean his condition had been worse than most. She could just mean his emotional scars from the attack and his split with Dana had been more extensive than most. Or she could mean that she'd remembered him as he'd remembered her.

He stepped away. "I should be finished with this door

by the time it takes you to make a stir-fry. We could have a race."

"Or we could take our time and not worry about who finishes first," she suggested.

Yep, he liked this woman's positive vision of the world. He just wondered when, exactly, he'd lost his.

During lunch, Jase kept the conversation light, mostly answering questions Sara had about the vineyard and the types of wine it produced. After Amy finished, she scrambled from her chair and curled up with her new stuffed toy, paging through a picture book.

"So she's in The Mommy Club's day care program while you work?" Jase asked.

"Yes, she is. The staff are wonderful."

"I didn't realize until after a discussion with Marissa that she takes her little boy, Jordan, there, too." His assistant had told him The Mommy Club day care program allowed for a sliding scale according to a parent's income. "Marissa doesn't seem to worry with Jordan there."

"I think Kaitlyn was involved in hiring the staff," Sara explained. "What I like is that I can stop in on my lunch hour. In the fall, Amy will be in kindergarten and I'll have to figure out what to do when she gets off school."

"Being a parent is never easy, is it? And being a single parent has to be doubly tough."

Sara didn't seem to want to comment on that and he wondered if she ever openly discussed her marriage. Her husband had been the manager of a home improvement store, but Jase didn't know more than that about him. Sara didn't seem to be in the mood to confide. In a flash, he remembered Dana and her penchant for keeping feelings and motives and even her life on assignments to herself. Most of all, he remembered her betrayal and easy desertion. He really should stay far away from Sara and her marriage and her past. His own past had forged who he was. Maybe everyone had secrets and stories they didn't want to tell.

Picking up his plate, he stood and said, "I'll help you clean up."

But Sara stood, too. "No, of course not. You fixed my windows and screen door and I don't want to keep you from the rest of your day."

Subtext: she was ready for him to leave.

He did carry his plate to the sink and set it there. With a glance at Amy, he noticed she'd fallen asleep, Moppy tucked under her arm, the picture book open beside her on the sofa.

"Does she still take naps?" he asked.

"Only when they catch her unaware."

He smiled. "That would make a wonderful photograph. Almost makes me want to get out my camera again."

"You don't take photos anymore? You're so good at it!"

He gave her a wry look. "I haven't since I came home. Too many memories about the last ones I took." Those photos had been shot in the refugee camp the day of the attack.

"You can't let what happened take away your gift."

That was one way of looking at it, he supposed.

"I'll walk you out," Sara suggested.

She followed him as he opened the screen door, which now hung correctly on its hinges. Outside the cottage, with the scent of roses climbing on a trellis beside the house redolent, he stared down at her, the desire to kiss her so strong he could taste it.

But instead he did the best thing for both of them. He picked up the toolbox he'd left outside the door and said, "Goodbye, Sara." He could feel her gaze on his back as he walked away.

## Chapter Three

Amy ran from Sara's side before she could catch her.

Her daughter's giggles reinforced Sara's resolve that she'd done the right thing by moving to the vineyard a few days ago. But when she saw where Amy was headed, she wondered about her decision all over again.

Jase was standing near a vine-laced trellis, his T-shirt pulling tightly across his shoulder muscles. He was tanned and fit and gave off an eminently masculine air. Especially with more than a day's beard stubbling his jaw.

When he saw Amy running toward him, he caught her, swung her around and made her giggle more.

He'd make a wonderful dad.

Sara banished the errant thought almost as quickly as it had entered her head and ran over to her daughter. She and Jase hadn't talked since their impromptu dinner. He'd come and gone, she'd come and gone, and they'd passed like two ships in the night, neither sure where they were headed. But Jase looked sure now.

"She has more energy than a high-speed train," he remarked with a wry smile.

"And she's just as fast. All I have to do is blink and she's into something she shouldn't be. Sorry if she bothered you."

"No bother. That's the nice thing about a vineyard. It's a big place. Are you settled in?"

"We are."

The way he was looking at her made her wish she'd combed her hair. She'd changed into shorts and a T-shirt when she'd gotten home from work and now she felt as if his eyes saw everything.

"Come on," he said. "I'll give you a tour. Maybe Amy can walk off some of that energy."

With Amy only a few feet away, Sara focused her attention on the vined trellises rather than on Jase. The trellis system was set up with about twelve feet between the rows and approximately eight feet between vines. "I've never tasted Raintree wines."

"We'll have to set you up for a wine tasting. We're the best in the state, but then of course I'm prejudiced. Our tasting host is on vacation right now. But he'll be back at the end of the week."

"Tasting host?"

"Tony works closely with Liam, keeps an eye on inventory and handles tours around the vineyard."

Amy had run up ahead, her attention taken by a stone on the ground.

"Did you ever consider staying here instead of writing and photographing the four corners of the world?"

"No. I felt I had to succeed on my own."

"Did your father want you to stay?"

Jase cocked his head. "He did. But I needed space… and something different. As a teenager, I read about every place on earth I wanted to see, and I saw causes that needed advocates, especially for kids who were displaced. After college, I found my niche with photojournalism. My editors liked the fact that I could write as well as shoot pics in hot spots." After a pause, he said, "You're too easy to talk to. I never revisit my past if I can help it."

"I don't have magic powers," she said with a smile.

"No, but your genuine interest is addictive."

Was she genuinely interested in Jase Cramer? Glancing at her daughter, remembering her marriage—the highs and lows, the plunge into discord—she knew she shouldn't be.

Suddenly the sound of a car engine preceded a vehicle along the driveway that led to the cottage. Sara studied the black sedan as it parked next to her car in the gravel area beside the trellis.

"Were you expecting someone?" Jase asked.

"No. Maybe it's someone here on vineyard business."

Even as she spoke, she doubted her theory. No one would be coming in the early evening, and besides, the parking lot for the winery was clearly marked by a sign that led visitors there rather than to the cottage.

Jase waited as a short man with wire-rimmed glasses climbed out of the sedan. "I don't recognize him. Let's go see what he wants."

Sara beckoned to Amy and then captured her hand, swinging it between them. At the door to her cottage, she faced the man who wore a three-piece suit and bow tie.

"Mrs. Stevens?" he asked, pleasantly enough.

"Yes, I'm Sara Stevens, and this is Jase Cramer."

"Pleased to meet you. I'm Ross Kiplinger, from High Point Insurance. I've come to ask you a few questions about the house and the fire. This might take a little while. Maybe we could go inside and sit down?"

Sara supposed they'd have to go over the policy Conrad had taken out on their house when he'd bought it.

"I can take Amy on a walk, if you'd like," Jase offered. "But we'll stay within shouting distance if you need us. Can we see some ID?" Jase asked the man.

Kiplinger didn't look put out at all, just took his wallet from his pocket and opened it to his driver's license. Then he took a security ID badge from an inside pocket. He showed them that, too. "I'm not an ax murderer," he assured them. "I have a briefcase inside my car that has Mrs. Stevens's policy inside, if you'd like to see that, too."

Sara believed he was who he said he was. She crouched down in front of Amy. "Would you like to go for a walk with Mr. Jase?"

Amy glanced down at the stone in her hand, then up at Jase. "Can we find more stones?"

"We can collect as many as you want." He held out his hand to her and she took it.

As Jase and her daughter walked off, Sara wished she was going with them, rather than stepping inside with Ross Kiplinger. But the sooner she received her fire insurance settlement, the sooner she and Amy would have a normal life again…the sooner they would leave Raintree Winery.

Jase and Amy traipsed along the trellises, looking for anything interesting to explore. Amy was entranced by the shape of a leaf, the length of a vine shoot, a tiny yellow flower that was simply a weed. He knew caring for a child was a heavy responsibility, but he imagined that the joy of living with one could balance that out. All those years he had taken pictures of kids, he hadn't really considered being a dad himself, maybe because he knew nothing about lasting relationships. Maybe because since he'd returned home, the taste of the betrayal was still too bitter in his mouth. Dana's involvement with another man while they were engaged, her desertion when he was at his lowest, still stirred resentment he'd like to rid himself of. Most days he pushed the past away and it stayed packed in the boxes up in the attic along with his cameras. But, for some reason, inviting Sara to the vineyard had unearthed much of it.

Sound carried across the vineyard and he heard the rumble of the black car's engine as it started up. Kiplinger had been with Sara close to an hour.

Amy was stooped on the ground, her red-brown hair falling over her shoulders as she studied a bug crawling through the dirt. He crouched down beside her.

"That's a busy bug, but I think we're going to have to leave him for now. I bet your mom's missing you."

Amy looked up at Jase. "She cries sometimes. I don't want her to cry."

Out of the mouths of babes. Did Sara cry because she missed her husband? Did she still love him? Or had losing everything in the fire caused her tears to flow? She gave the impression that she was strong and could handle anything, but at night, when she was alone, what thoughts ran through her head?

"We wouldn't want to make her cry. Come on, let's go back and make her smile. I bet she always smiles when she sees you."

It only took them about ten minutes to make their way through the rows and find the path that led to the cottage. All was quiet as they approached. Jase was actually a little surprised that Sara didn't come to meet them. A shout across the vineyard rows, and she would have known where they were.

Jase could see Sara through the screen door. She was sitting on the sofa, staring into space.

Amy pulled open the door and ran toward her, holding out the stones in her little hand.

"Mommy, look what I found."

Sara immediately took her daughter into her arms, gave her a hug and said, "Let me see."

But Jase could tell the sound of her voice was forced. He could see her smile wobble. What had gone on with that insurance investigator?

"We'll have to put your stones in a box. We'll make it a treasure box."

"I'll put it under my bed."

"That's a great idea. But right now we have to get you washed up and ready for bed. Jase, thanks for taking her on a walk."

"I need to snitch one of your bottles of water. Why don't you put Amy to bed, and then we can talk about your visitor."

Sara's eyes grew wide and she looked almost fearful. "There's no need—"

"I think there is. You look a little shaken up and I'd like to know why."

She glanced down at Amy. "Honey, why don't you go wash your hands and brush your teeth. I'll be in in a minute."

"Are you going to look for a box?"

"I will. Go on, now."

When Amy had left the room, Sara squared her shoulders. "I'm fine, Jase. Really. There's no need for you to stay."

Should he push, or shouldn't he? "I'm going to drink that bottle of water. After you put Amy to bed, if you want me to leave, I will. It's your call."

Her lower lip trembled a little but then she firmed it up and gave him a resigned look. "Fine. It usually takes about twenty minutes. If you get tired of waiting…"

"I won't."

Sara avoided his gaze and went to help her daughter prepare for bed.

Jase stood at the counter, drinking his bottle of water. He didn't want to crowd Sara. If she wanted him to go, he'd go. If she wanted him to stay, he'd listen, just as she'd listened to him two years ago.

When she returned to the living room, he really wasn't sure what her decision would be. Her expression was as worried as it had been when he and Amy had returned from their walk.

At first, she looked at him and said, "You might not want to get involved in my life."

"Listening won't involve me."

Her pretty brows hiked up as if to say, *You don't believe that any more than I do.*

He shrugged. Then he set his water bottle down and crossed the room to her, settling his hands on her shoulders. "Maybe I can help."

"No one can help with this. Mr. Kiplinger was here to warn me they might not be paying out on my policy. He didn't put it into so many words, but the insurance company believes I could have set the fire."

Nothing had prepared Jase for that, but he didn't step away. He just responded, "Why don't you tell me what's going on."

Her voice almost a whisper, Sara said, "I don't talk about my marriage."

He dropped his hands from her shoulders. "Maybe you should."

"I'm sure you don't like to talk about your fiancée calling off your engagement."

Whoa! So she knew how to fight when the time came. "It was a mutual decision when I found out she was unfaithful. Was your husband unfaithful?"

Sara looked around the room for a minute as if she were trying to find a corner to escape to, as if anything would be better than telling him about this. But then she took a deep breath and motioned to the sofa. "Let's sit."

"It's a long story?" he joked lightly.

"It's…complicated."

*What relationship wasn't?* he thought.

After they were seated on the couch, she turned toward him, her eyes a little too bright. "When Conrad and I first married, I moved into his apartment because his was bigger than mine. He managed a home-improvement store and it was doing well. My job was secure, so we didn't have to think about finances very much. But then he entered into talks to open a store of his own. He spoke with bankers and investors, had a couple of custom suits made and his taste in suits, shoes and wine changed, becoming more expensive. I loved him. I trusted him. I thought he could do no wrong so I went along with the changes. Then I got pregnant."

"Unplanned?" Jase asked.

She tilted her hand back and forth. "We wanted kids. We just weren't sure when we wanted to start a family. We went away one weekend and the pregnancy was the result."

Jase found himself not wanting to think about Sara with another man. That was crazy. Conrad had been her husband.

"What happened after your pregnancy?"

"Conrad thought we should buy a house. He was sure the investors for his own store were going to come through.

We looked at several houses and there was one we really liked. I thought the price was too high, but Conrad said we could afford it. I wasn't privy to all of his business dealings, so I believed him. He took care of the paperwork and settled on the house. I knew the mortgage payment each month seemed exorbitant but Conrad said we could manage it, and I shouldn't worry. I was seven months pregnant then, and concerned about everything baby. The thought of planning the nursery and the baby's playroom and decorating the rest of the house kept me more occupied than I should have been. I should have asked more questions, but I was a trusting wife."

Jase heard the bitterness behind the words and suspected what was coming. What was it about loving someone that made a woman put good sense aside and wear blinders? He was a good one to pass judgment on that. Maybe men weren't much different.

Because Sara had sounded angrier at herself than she did at her husband, he asked, "What didn't you see?"

"I didn't see that we were sinking deeper and deeper into debt. I didn't see that Conrad's store wasn't doing as well as he said it was. I didn't see that his deals with investors never materialized. I didn't see that the expensive cars and the diamond bracelet he gave me for my birthday were just a sham to cover up everything that was happening."

"You found out about all this after your husband died?"

"No. That wasn't the way it happened. The way it happened made everything worse. Men came to the house one evening and repossessed Conrad's car. Amy was two and I had gone back to work part-time because I really do love what I do. That night I started asking questions and didn't stop, questions I should have asked a lot sooner. I found out we were so deep in debt I didn't see how we were ever going to get out. Conrad had lied about so much. There were *no* investors. Anyone he'd tried to convince decided the economy was too weak. The store he managed *wasn't* doing well. Our credit cards had reached their limit. I just felt so…betrayed that he kept it all from me."

"Once trust is broken, it's difficult to earn back."

"Exactly. I found I couldn't trust him. I didn't know when to believe him. I had doubts about everything he said. That was our marriage for the next year—all filled with tension, regret and resentment. I went back to work full-time and found The Mommy Club day care instead of a private child care provider. I covered home budget costs wherever I could. But then I found out Conrad was still courting investors for a store that would never be! He was running up bar tabs and dinner tabs that we couldn't afford. He thought I wasn't supporting his dreams. I thought he wasn't facing reality. And then, after a year of living like that, Conrad had a heart attack in his office at work. It was a massive coronary and he couldn't be revived. The doctors said there was a defect that was probably congenital and Conrad never knew he had it, but I think the stress did it. Our marriage did it. *I* did it."

Her voice broke and Jase realized how much all of it still affected her. He also understood what he saw in Sara's eyes so often wasn't just grief for her husband, but guilt for his death. That was a heavy burden to carry.

He wanted to cover her hand with his, yet tonight that didn't seem right, not while they were talking about her husband. "His death wasn't your fault. He brought everything on by his dishonesty."

"*I* brought everything on by not probing and pushing and opening my eyes to what was happening."

"Sara, you were a young mother with a new baby. You trusted your husband. That's not a sin."

"Maybe not, but it sure was a flaw. If I had demanded to

be part of the financial planning as we bought the house, or even after Amy was born, everything would have been different."

"Maybe. Maybe not. If your husband was a spender then he was a spender, and he might have needed help to curb the habit. Determination sometimes isn't enough. It's not much different from a drug addict, knowing she should stop and yet she can't."

Sara looked at him curiously when he said that, but he stopped there. He wasn't about to go on. They were talking about Sara, not about him, and that's the way he'd like to keep it. He'd been in his twenties before he'd finally come to terms with the fact that he was ashamed of his childhood, ashamed of how he'd ended up at Raintree in the first place. He didn't tell anyone about that. His father didn't talk about it, either, with good reason. How could he be proud of Jase—born illegitimate, his father unknown and his mother a drug addict? That wasn't something Ethan liked to tell his friends. That wasn't something that he'd ever *told* his friends.

Jase focused on Sara. "Looking at your situation practically, wasn't it better after Conrad died?"

"Jase! How could you say such a thing?" She looked horrified at his putting the obvious into words.

"You know exactly what I mean. What happened with the debt?"

"Most things weren't paid off and we still owed, not just the house that was dropping in value every day, but the furniture and the rugs and the wall paintings. After Conrad died, all the debt was left to me. He'd canceled his life insurance policy because he couldn't make the payments, so I sold what I could—jewelry, rugs, art. I couldn't sell the house because it had depreciated so much. All I could do was try to keep up with the mortgage payments.

Amy and I had a roof over our heads, but I bought day-old bread, pasta on special and didn't drive anywhere I didn't have to. Thank goodness Amy was too young to realize what was going on."

"But children pick up a lot. She probably understood that you were worried all of the time."

"Yes, I was."

"But your husband kept the fire insurance on the house."

"He had to. It was required by the mortgage company. So the house was heavily insured and that's why the insurance investigator is asking me tons of questions. It's why he thinks I burned down my house to dig myself out of a hole."

When Sara looked up at Jase, he knew she wasn't going to ask the question out loud, but he could hear it, anyway. *Do you think I would do such a thing?*

His immediate reaction was, *No, I don't.* Sara wasn't that kind of woman. On the other hand, he'd been wrong about a woman before. Exactly how well did he know Sara? He'd invited her here on gut instinct, but now his gut instinct was also telling him to be cautious.

All he said was, "I'm sorry you have to go through this."

She looked disappointed, maybe even hurt, and he didn't know what to do about that. But he wasn't about to become recklessly involved with her. That would be tantamount to marching into war without knowing where the enemy hid…to photographing refugee children without realizing they could all be victims of an attack.

No matter how much he wanted to put the past behind him, it constantly tapped him on the shoulder. Sara's past would do the same. Her husband had lied to her and put their family in a situation no family should be in. She'd apparently loved him but she'd had to live with doubts while she tried to make her marriage work…while she'd tried to forgive what he'd done. Then he'd left her with a mess.

"Did Kiplinger say what happens next?"

"I wait."

"Don't let your thoughts bury you," Jase advised her. "This could turn out all right in the end. It just might take a while to get settled."

"If I'm here longer than a month, I'm going to pay you rent."

"Sara, that's not necessary."

"Yes, it is. I don't want your father to think I'm taking advantage of your hospitality."

"If you're here a month, then we'll talk about it." Jase rose to his feet, wanting to take her into his arms, yet knowing that wasn't the prudent thing to do. "Now, you've got to get some sleep for work tomorrow."

"You make this sound as if it's not serious."

"I know it's serious."

When he gazed into her eyes, he felt a startling sexual arousal that hadn't plagued him for a very long time. But he willed it under control and he knew the best thing for both of them was for him to leave.

After she rose and walked him to the door, again the same question was in her eyes. *Do you believe I would do such a thing?*

But he couldn't answer her now. He couldn't let his guard down long enough to sort it all out. But he did run his thumb down her cheek, relishing the softness of it. He did say, "We'll talk again. Soon."

Then he walked away.

The following evening, Amy held on to Sara's hand tightly as her mother led her up the flagstone pathway to the vineyard's office building. She still hadn't met Raintree's chief winemaker, Liam Corbett. His comings and goings were at different times than hers. She'd come over to the offices today to see Jase's assistant. Marissa had watched over Amy on moving day. Since then they had chatted a few times. Sara felt comfortable with her and today she needed some advice from an insider at the vineyard. She could have left already, Sara knew, but her little boy, Jordan, was still at The Mommy Club day care when she'd picked up Amy. Sara was hoping she could catch her if she was working late.

She stooped down to Amy. "This won't take too long, and I'll make your favorite supper when we get back— burgers and French fries. But you have to eat a little bit of broccoli, too."

"Dipped in cheese?"

Sara smiled. "You've got it."

Amy's Mary Janes tapped on the Mexican tile as they approached the first office in the long hallway. Located beside the winery, this was the hub of Raintree's business activity. Windows allowed Sara to see Marissa inside the first office. She was waiting at the printer, collecting documents as they spewed out. She was a beautiful woman, a couple of years younger than Sara. Her hair was the deepest brown and curly. Her chocolate-brown eyes were as expressive as her wide mouth, and she didn't hide what she was thinking. Right now, Sara needed her opinion.

There was a walkway through Marissa's office that led to a much bigger office beyond. Sara suspected that was where Jase usually sat, at the massive mahogany desk. There were double file cabinets behind it and beautiful paintings of Carmel and Big Sur. His chairs as well as his desk blotter were wine-colored leather. The wood paneling was as fine as the Oriental rug on the floor.

The printer stopped spewing out paper and Sara

knocked lightly. Marissa's face broke into a wide smile. "Sara, it's so good to see you. You, too, Amy. How do you like your new room?"

Amy stayed close to Sara, then peeked out around her legs. "I like it."

Marissa laughed. "Well, good." Her attention went back to Sara. "Are you feeling more at home here?"

"I am, but that's what I'd like to talk to you about. First, let me ask if I'm tying you up. I don't want to keep you from picking up your son."

"I often work late, but now and then, Jase will give me a whole afternoon off. It evens out. He had new orders come in tonight that I had to organize and give to the account manager."

Sara took a few folded sheets of paper and crayons from her purse. "Do you mind if Amy sits on the floor to draw?"

"She doesn't have to sit on the floor. Come here, pumpkin. Sit up here at my desk." She took hold of a pump at the side of the chair and gave it a few squeezes. The chair rose a few inches, making it easier for Amy to draw. "Okay, there?"

Amy nodded.

Marissa motioned Sara toward the file cabinets. "What can I do for you?"

"The cottage is wonderful," Sara assured her quickly. "Jase has been welcoming. But I don't want to take advantage of living here. The problem is, there could be a delay with the insurance money on the house."

"Red tape?"

Marissa's question was an honest one. She felt more like a friend than a stranger. Should she be honest with her?

"You look troubled about something," Marissa noticed. She was obviously perceptive, too. "I am. The insurance company is investigating the fire because I had a lot of debt."

"Who doesn't?"

"Mine was substantial, so substantial I believe they think I set the fire."

"Oh, no! You can't be serious."

"I am. No one knows about this besides Jase, so I'd appreciate it if you could keep it a secret."

"Of course, I can. What do you need from me?"

"I wondered if you know the best place to look for rental properties. I'd even consider a couple of rooms in someone's house. I want to keep the cost as low as I can. My main problem is moving Amy again. She really is settling in and likes it here. What would you do if it were you and Jordan?"

"If it were me and Jordan, I think I'd stay as long as I could. The vineyard is a beautiful place for Amy to play… a beautiful place to get your footing again. I'm sure Jase doesn't mind your being here."

"I don't know."

Marissa swept her hair back over her shoulder and studied Sara. "He seemed welcoming when you moved in. Besides, when a man and woman who have chemistry are in the same room, anyone can tell."

"Oh, no! There's nothing going on between us. My mind was on Amy and—"

"Tell me you didn't see how fine Jase looked as he moved in that sofa. Tell me you didn't notice how gray his eyes are, how his hair falls over his brow, that there's still that wanderlust element around him that makes a girl want to just run away with him."

"Are you thinking of running away with him?" Sara asked, partly as a defense, partly because she wanted to know.

"No, he's not my type. I'm attracted to the bad boys, the ones who love 'em and leave 'em."

Taking a stab in the dark, Sara guessed, "Jordan's father was one of those?"

After a brief hesitation, Marissa nodded. "He absolutely was, and it wasn't like I didn't know what I was getting into. I just wasn't careful enough."

"I'm trying to be careful," Sara assured her. "I have to, for Amy's sake. Chemistry is fine, but when there's no future beyond it—"

"You don't have to tell me about that. I know. You have to be Amy's future, and I have to be Jordan's. But there is another side to that. Sometimes we want to be independent women and accept no help from anyone else. That just makes our lives harder. The Mommy Club found me my position here with Jase. It was a gift from heaven because I could get insurance benefits from working here in order to pay my bills when Jordan was born. At first it seemed too good to be true. But Jase had looked at my high school transcript. He liked what he saw. My boss at the restaurant where I was waitressing gave me a good recommendation. He said I was a hard worker, so Jase decided to take a chance on me. It was a gift I accepted. You should consider the cottage a gift you should accept, too. You'll know when the time's right to leave."

"I owe The Mommy Club so much. Is there anything I can do now to start paying them back?"

"Sure. You can help out at the food drive on Saturday."

She remembered the event Kaitlyn had told her about when she'd moved in. "Can I bring Amy?"

"Sure. It's at the day care center. A couple of volunteers will keep the kids occupied so we can work."

"What time?"

"We're starting early, around 8:00 a.m., but when you

get there, you get there. I'm hoping we'll have so many hands, it will all get organized quickly."

"You can count on me to be there."

The two women moved closer to the desk again and looked at the picture Amy had drawn. Right away they could see she'd drawn a tall male stick figure in blue jeans and a T-shirt. She'd drawn herself beside him in a pink shirt and shorts. She was lopsided but recognizable. Her stick fingers were on top of Jase's. Beside them, she'd drawn a long green vine.

"Jase took Amy for a walk while the investigator talked to me," Sara explained. "I think she had a good time."

"Maybe you and Jase should go for a walk," Marissa suggested with a sly look in her eye.

"No, I'm not going to encourage…chemistry. My life is just too unsettled right now."

"Chemistry could be fun," Marissa said with a twinkle in her eyes.

But Sara knew chemistry could also blow up in her face.

## Chapter Four

The rest of the week passed quickly as Sara helped her patients recover from injuries, build up strength after surgeries and resume function after a debilitating stroke. Her work kept her focused but every now and then she thought about what Marissa had said. Could others sense an attraction between her and Jase? Was he as attracted to her as she was to him?

She was still asking herself that question among others—like, *Did Jase believe she could have set the fire?*—as she sorted through a box of donated groceries Saturday morning at the day care center. Carrying the box across the room to station three where the canned vegetables were being stored, she smiled at Kaitlyn who seemed to work tirelessly in her practice as well as help parents whenever she could. With her blond hair and green eyes, Kaitlyn should be on the cover of a magazine rather than trying to make kids laugh when she used her stethoscope.

"I think we have enough canned vegetables for an army," Sara told her now.

"I'm hoping some of the growers will donate fresh produce, too. The kids will go for carrots and celery sticks. Amy looks as if she's having fun."

Glancing over to the corner of the room where the four-, five- and six-year-olds were playing games with Marissa and other volunteers, Sara had to agree. "Candyland is one of her favorite games."

"I wonder if I could come up with a board game with vegetables on it," Kaitlyn joked.

Sara was about to reply when a newcomer entered the center. Her heart began pounding faster as Jase carried a large carton of canned goods toward them.

"I didn't expect him to be here," Sara murmured, feeling suddenly off balance.

After a quick glance at her, Kaitlyn explained, "Jase offered to pick up food for us at other drop-off points."

When Jase's gaze met Sara's, he stopped for a moment. She wasn't sure what was going to happen next…if he was just going to drop the box on the table and walk away, or if he was actually going to talk to her. Why did she suddenly feel like a teenager in high school?

Except a teenager in high school wouldn't have to worry about an insurance investigation or a marriage that had turned out so much differently than Sara had wanted… or expected.

Kaitlyn's smile was wide as she greeted Jase and then asked, "So how did we do?"

"My truck is full. Do you want it all on this table?"

"Are you going to stick around after you bring it in?"

"I can. What do you need?"

After Kaitlyn scanned the room to check on the progress of her volunteers, she said, "I have a list of the families who will be accepting donations. You and Sara could start boxing, if that's okay with the two of you."

What could Sara say? "That's fine."

Kaitlyn pointed to a stack of coupons on the table. "Don't forget to include one of those for each family. The coupon will enable them to take home a free turkey or ham."

"Got it," Jase said. "I'll empty the truck and we'll get started."

Once Kaitlyn gave Sara the list, Sara began the packaging process. After lining up twenty cartons on the floor, she added an assortment of fruits and vegetables and packaged goods to each box, checking expiration dates. Though she was aware of Jase coming and going, she kept her mind on what she was doing until...

He stood beside her and asked, "How can I help?"

He could help by having a real conversation with her, by assuring her he would never believe she'd set fire to her own house!

Instead she pointed to the carton she was attempting to fill. "Just grab some of each food group—vegetables, fruits, proteins—and put three or four in each box. It's not a lot, but it will help. When I think about how The Mommy Club stocked my refrigerator after I moved in—" She stopped as her throat tightened and her eyes grew misty.

Jase studied her as if he was trying to figure something out. His scrutiny was unsettling and she tried to turn away, but he wouldn't let her. His large hand capped her shoulder and nudged her toward him again. "We have to talk, Sara, but this isn't the place."

She wondered what he wanted to talk about. Maybe his father wanted to evict her from the cottage. Maybe Jase did. But she wouldn't let him see her worry. She wouldn't let him see that his opinion mattered...because it shouldn't.

"You know where I'm staying," she said lightly, and tried to smile. She thought he was going to say more, maybe give her a hint as to what he was thinking.

However, a couple came in and the man called to Jase. "How did you get roped into this? Connie convinced me she needed my man power." The man and woman were both carrying grocery bags full of food. They set them on the table, then approached Jase and Sara.

"It's a good cause," Jase said. He quickly made introductions. "Tony and Connie Russo, this is Sara Stevens. She's staying in our cottage. Sara, Tony is our wine-tasting host and Liam's right-hand man. Connie teaches kids how to ride on their ranch." He turned back to the couple. "I didn't know you were involved with The Mommy Club."

"I learned about it from one of the parents," Connie explained. "We usually help with the food drives."

"Teaching kids horseback riding must be such fun," Sara commented. "I'd love to watch sometime. When I treat children, I often wish I had something other than the regular exercises, games and swimming to offer to them. Riding could teach them balance and self-confidence."

At Connie's raised brows, Jase explained, "Sara's a physical therapist."

"Who says social media's the only place to link up anymore?" Connie joked.

They all laughed, and Sara began to feel more comfortable with the couple.

"I brought the crew cab today," Tony said. "We could deliver some of these on the way home."

"Where are the kids?" Jase asked.

"They're with my sister," Connie explained.

"How old are your kids?" Sara asked.

"Rena is nine and Marie is eleven."

"You're into dangerous tween territory," Sara warned.

"Don't I know it! Tony is the one who's having a little trouble with that."

Her husband held up his hand in a stop sign. "Oh, no. We're not having that discussion in mixed company. If you want to speak to Sara about bras and 'the talk,' I'm going to head over to Kaitlyn and find out if she wants me to load up these filled cartons."

Connie playfully punched her husband in the arm right before he hurried off. "He talks like he doesn't want to be involved, but he does."

"I'll start stacking these by the door," Jase told the women as he hefted a box into his arms and carried it to the other side of the room.

"The cottage on Raintree has been empty for a while," Connie noted. "I got the impression Ethan didn't want anyone but Liam and Jase on the property."

"I'm only there temporarily. There was a fire and I didn't have anywhere to go."

"You're *that* Sara Stevens. I heard the news spot on the radio. I'm sorry. It must be awful to lose everything."

"Oh, but I didn't. I have my daughter and she's what's most important." Sara pointed to Amy who was laughing and giggling with one of the other kids.

"Were you Jase's physical therapist when he returned from Africa?"

"Yes, I was. That's how we met."

"No wonder he asked you to stay at the cottage. I know he owes you a lot."

Connie and Tony must be good friends with Jase if he told them about his therapy.

"He worked hard to get better. He doesn't owe me anything."

When Jase returned to Sara and Connie, he said, "I'm going to have to get going, too, but I can deliver some of these along the way, and the rest of you can concentrate on the summer lunch program."

Sara was hoping he'd stay, that maybe they could start their discussion here even though he said it wasn't the best place. But that wasn't going to happen. Winery business was calling.

The men loaded boxes into both trucks, and then Connie and Tony left. After checking in with Kaitlyn, Jase stopped at Sara's station again.

"They're a nice couple," she said.

"Unlike a lot of other marriages, theirs seems to work. Tony and I cross paths fairly often. They're good friends. I was surprised to see them here. Yet I shouldn't be. Connie is all about helping kids." He paused and looked at his watch. "Well, I'd better get going. I have a meeting and I don't want to be late. I'll see you back at the vineyard," he told Sara, his intense gaze making his words a promise.

The wine cellar was a perfect fifty-five degrees late Saturday evening. It was also silent and a world away from the rest of the vineyard. Jase studied a row of tilted racks until he found first one bottle of wine, a Pinot Noir, and then another, a Merlot. He thought about seeing Sara this morning. He couldn't get her off his mind. He was going to keep his word to her. They were going to have a talk.

The heavy wooden door to the basement room creaked and Jase was surprised to see his father walk in. He was holding a clipboard.

"I thought you'd retired for the night." Often his father ate his dinner in his room, then stayed there for the rest of the evening.

"No, I was talking to Liam about this year's crop. How was your meeting earlier with the marketing company?"

"It went well. I think they're what we need. They'll

start building our brand on social media, as well as in traditional advertising."

"Build our brand," Ethan scoffed. "We've had a brand for seventy years."

"We have. But branding is different now. It's about catchphrases, memorable sound bites, reaching the most people with the smallest amount of effort."

"Go with them, then, if you think they'll agree with our marketing budget."

"What are you doing down here so late?" Jase asked.

"Checking off the wine I want to use for the party next weekend. Don't forget to dust the mothballs off your tux."

Every June his father hosted a soiree that brought together vineyard owners, neighbors and any contacts his father found beneficial. It was black tie and evening wear all the way.

Ethan nodded to the bottles of wine in Jase's hand. "Private party?"

How much to say? "No, just a small wine tasting. Sara's never had Raintree wine."

Ethan's brows drew together. "If you give her too much attention, she's not going to want to leave."

"Attention? We're going to talk and have a glass of wine."

"How do you know she's not a gold digger?"

Jase sighed. "Don't start."

"She's down on her luck, and maybe ready to reach for anything she can get, including you."

"You think I'm such a good catch?" he tried to make a joke of it, but as usual, Ethan wasn't in a joking mood.

"You'll have an inheritance any woman would want."

"Sara isn't interested in my inheritance." He wasn't even sure she was interested in *him,* not after what she'd gone through with her husband.

"She'd be a fool not to be. So how long is she staying? Have you gotten a date from her yet?"

Jase hesitated, debating with himself about how much to say. He knew the truth was best. "It might be a little longer than she planned. Her insurance settlement might be delayed."

"Why?"

"She had debt and a high mortgage. The insurance company is investigating."

"And you don't think she's a gold digger," Ethan muttered.

"I think she's a single mom caught in circumstances she can't control. I'll see you in the morning."

He wouldn't get drawn into an argument about Sara or about anything else. He knew from experience his father didn't change his mind once he'd made it up. Jase had had practice standing his ground the past two years. Sara wouldn't be an exception.

When Jase knocked on Sara's door ten minutes later, he didn't know what to expect. Amy might be in bed or she might not be. Either way, it was fine with him. Just thinking of her created an ache inside him. She reminded him of a dream that had slipped away.

Sara came to the door dressed in shorts and a tank top for an evening at home with her daughter, her arms full of toys. Her hair was clipped on top of her head, strands escaping in a way that made Jase want to touch them. He wanted to touch *her*.

Instead he offered her the bottles of wine. "I thought we could have a tasting and see what you like. If you're free…"

"Amy's in bed, and I'm just about finished cleaning up her toys." She put the armload in a plastic bin, then turned back to him. "I don't have wineglasses, but I do have juice glasses."

"They'll do." He opened the screen door and carried the bottles to the coffee table. "I even brought a corkscrew. Just in case you didn't have one."

"Good thinking, or your wine tasting would have fizzled."

He gazed into her eyes and felt that elemental attraction again. So elemental that he reminded himself he was here to *talk* to her.

After Jase removed the banding around the bottle caps and used the corkscrew, he poured a sample of the first bottle of wine into two of the four juice glasses. "How long were you at the day care center?"

"We finished around three."

He picked up one of the glasses and handed it to her. "I'm terrifically impressed with The Mommy Club. After I left there today, I had an idea about promoting it more, to get more people involved."

"What's your idea?" Sara's fingers brushed his when she took the glass. She was looking at him as if what he had to say was more important than taking a drink.

Damn, but he wanted to kiss her.

"Try your wine," he said, his voice husky.

She took a whiff of it first and then a small sip. He could tell she let it linger on her tongue a bit. This wine tasting might have been a very bad idea, especially if they didn't just gulp it right down, which a good wine connoisseur never did.

"It's drier than I like," she said honestly.

"Okay, then let's try the next one."

"Aren't you going to tell me your idea?"

"I want to get you set up with the right wine first. But

if you want a really sweet wine, I should have brought a dessert wine."

"You have those, too?"

"Sure. We make a raspberry that's great over ice, but in the meantime, try this." He poured from the second bottle into the other two juice glasses.

This time, after she took a sip, she smiled. "Perfect."

"You mean you might have more than a sip?"

She took another swallow and smiled again. "Yep, I could probably drink two glasses of this."

"Just two?"

"I don't drink much, so when I do, it goes to my head."

He was going to have to remember that because if he ever kissed her, he wanted her totally sober. He cut that thought off and reverted back to his idea about The Mommy Club. "If there was more publicity about The Mommy Club, good publicity, more people would volunteer, right?"

"That makes sense. I know Kaitlyn tries to get the word out, but that's not always easy."

"Exactly. The organization needs more than a website or flyers placed at strategic places. So I was thinking about going to Cal Hodgekins at the newspaper and pitching a series of articles on The Mommy Club."

"That's a wonderful idea! I would think any newspaper would be glad to print something you wrote. You won a Pulitzer. What more could any newspaper want?"

Sara's words brought back the award-winning series of articles he had written, the photo layout that had gone with them. Unfortunately, he remembered all too well why he'd stopped writing and stowed away his camera. The assault that day on the aid workers had been bloody, brutal and deadly for some. He'd been lucky. For some reason, his life had been spared. But the pictures in his head of what had happened that day would haunt him forever.

"Did I say something wrong?"

He brought his gaze up to hers. "No, you didn't. It's just been a long time since I've considered writing or photographing anything."

She looked as if she wanted to reach out to him, but maybe she was afraid to. Maybe her troubled marriage prevented her from reaching out to men. Or maybe Jase's lack of response when she'd told him about her husband had affected her.

With a small shrug, she suggested, "If you came up with this idea, and it stirs your journalistic instincts, maybe it's time to start again."

Perhaps that was true. Perhaps enough time had passed. Could the same be true for his libido, which had been in deep freeze since he'd confronted Dana about her infidelity?

Bringing Sara here had stirred it all up again. "I suppose avoidance isn't a viable strategy for living."

"Avoidance? Or denial?" she asked in that straightforward manner that he appreciated. "Because I've done both and neither helps. The more you bury the pain, the more it hurts."

"I never thought about it like that," he admitted. "Burying the pain seemed like a good idea, especially when my physical therapy was over. I don't know if I could have lived with it on a daily basis."

"And now?" Sara's golden-brown eyes were soft, her expression understanding of what he'd experienced.

"And now I don't think avoidance or denial will fix the problem."

"What problem do you want to fix?"

Her hand was toying with the juice glass on the coffee

table. Reaching over, he covered hers with his. "I shouldn't have left the other night the way I did."

She glanced down at their hands, then back up at him. "I dumped a lot of my personal history on you...and the news about the investigation."

"When I was your patient, I told you what happened with my fiancée."

"That was part of your therapy. It's important for me to listen carefully when I treat someone because not all physical pain is from a physical source."

After he absorbed that, he admitted, "I wanted to know about your marriage, and I still do. But I know it's painful for you to talk about."

"It is. But I want to let go of it, not dwell on it. Still, sometimes what happened with Conrad directs what I think about things now, how I feel about getting involved with someone again, if I should even consider it. Certainly not while I'm in the mess I'm in."

"You mean the insurance investigation?"

She pulled her hand away from his. "Yes. I saw the doubts in your eyes, Jase. Doubts anybody would have."

"I don't doubt you, Sara."

She looked wary. "But the way you left—"

"That avoidance I just spoke of—avoid pain, avoid involvement, avoid controversy. I've been pretty much doing that for two years, so that was my first response. I guess the bigger question was—did I want to get involved in your life by believing *anything* about you? Do you understand?"

"I think so."

He slid his hand along her neck and fingered her earlobe. She closed her eyes for a moment as if she enjoyed his touch, but then she opened them and he knew what he had to say.

"I don't for a minute believe you could set fire to your

own house. That's not you. That's not the woman who helped me heal. That's not the mom who takes care of Amy every day. So no matter what anyone else believes, know that I believe in you."

"Oh, Jase."

He knew moving in to kiss her was a mistake, especially after the history of pain they'd both experienced. But he felt urges he thought had died, and they were strong and couldn't be ignored. The look in her eyes told him she felt them, too.... The chemistry between them, the sexual hunger. That drove him further. He didn't know what he expected from her. He warned himself that he expected nothing.

But as soon as his lips took hers, fireworks burst bright and high. There were sparks and then fire that quickened every one of his nerve endings. The reason? She was kissing him back like she felt them, too.

As his tongue slid over hers, the taste of wine was heady. But even headier was her taste underneath, a sweetness that was pure woman. An alarm in the back of his head told him avoidance was still best, that remaining uninvolved was the safe way to go...that danger lurked in passion, the same way it lurked in the best cause.

But Sara smelled like strawberries and the sweetest garden mixture. As he ran his hands up and down her back, all he wanted to do was undress her.

That thought stalled when she abruptly ended the kiss, braced one hand against his chest and looked stricken.

"Amy's in the next room," she murmured, "and I...I can't do this."

This. Just what was *this?* Kissing until they stripped each other's clothes off? Having sex on her sofa while her daughter was in the next room? Becoming involved in a physical relationship that could hurt them both?

Like a mantra that needed to be recited in an interminable loop, he warned himself, *She's a mom. She doesn't sleep around. She deserves commitment.*

Being involved with Sara meant being involved with Amy. He wasn't father material. He'd never treat a child with the indifference with which Ethan had treated him, but what did he know about daily parenting? What did he know about having a relationship that lasted? That's exactly what Sara would want. But right now, he wasn't sure she wanted anything from him.

"I'm not tipsy," she assured him, "but I think you saying you believe me made me a little intoxicated."

He supposed that was as fitting an excuse as any, but he didn't like the fact she made an excuse. "I didn't say it so that would happen."

"I know," she almost whispered, moving a little bit farther away. Didn't she trust herself? Or didn't she trust him?

He stood. "I'm going to leave the wine. If you cork it, it will keep. You might develop a real taste for it."

"Jase, you understand why I stopped, don't you?"

He did, and he didn't. "I understand that sex can be different for a man and a woman, especially when there's a child involved. But I also think you need to admit your needs and not deny them."

"It's never just sex, Jase. Not for me. Is it for you?"

"Sometimes it is."

She looked disappointed at that, but what he said was the truth. It was the difference between them, and their lives—a difference that urged him toward the door. Although Sara followed him, he opened the screen door and stepped outside.

"Thanks for coming over tonight, Jase, and letting me know you believe me. That means a lot."

He gave her a smile that was hard to dredge up, nodded and left. Maybe avoidance was a virtue, after all.

"Are you sure you want to do that?" Marissa asked Sara late one afternoon as they stood in her office.

Sara had seen Marissa's car was still here and decided she could start paying back The Mommy Club one member at a time. She just didn't know if Marissa would go for it.

"Do what?" Jase asked, striding up the hall.

Sara had seen him go up to the house earlier and she was hoping he was still there. He must have gotten a bite to eat and come back to work.

Amy tugged on her hand. "I'm hungry, Mommy."

"I know, baby, just a couple of minutes."

Moving over to Amy, Jase waved a hand behind her ear and pulled out a coin. "Look what I found."

Amy's eyes lit up as if he'd done the most magical thing on earth. He handed it to her. "You can put it in your piggy bank. Do you have a piggy bank?"

"I have a doggy bank Miss Marissa gave me."

"That will do. If your mom stands here too long talking, maybe I can find another coin." He looked at Sara again. "So what are you two discussing? Or is it none of my business?"

"She wants to help me," Marissa said with a frown. "And she doesn't have to."

Jase's brows arched.

"I offered to pick up Jordan for her, that's all," Sara explained. "I'm already in town and I have to pick up Amy. I could bring Jordan here so she doesn't have to run in."

"Sounds like a good deal to me," Jase agreed, but Marissa was still frowning.

"If I let you do that for me, then you have to let me watch Amy if you need a babysitter. That would only be fair. And if I want to work late, I could just give you a call and tell you to leave Jordan at day care."

"Perfect." Sara was so mired in debt, she didn't want to be indebted any more, to anyone.

"And speaking of babysitters, you're both going to need one Saturday evening." Jase's smile was wide and did funny things to Sara's equilibrium.

Marissa snapped her fingers. "The Raintree Soiree."

"Yep. All the staff are invited, of course. But, Sara, I'd like you to come, too."

She wasn't exactly sure what kind of invitation this was. Was Jase asking her because she lived on the property? Or was he asking her because this was sort of a date?

"It's a glamorous event," Marissa said as if that would convince her.

But that just caused anxiety. "My wardrobe got wiped out."

"I know how to fix that," Marissa told her. "We'll talk."

Sara wasn't sure what Marissa had in mind, but she already knew she could trust her.

"It's settled, then." Jase waved his hand behind Amy's other ear. "Here you go. Thanks for being so patient while we talked."

Amy held a coin in each hand. "Look, Mommy, doggy-bank food."

They all laughed, but Sara was already nervous about Saturday night. She wished Jase's magic trick included an answer to the question of what she should do about *him*.

## Chapter Five

Sara was watching Amy plop a spoonful of chocolate chip cookie dough onto a baking sheet the following evening when there was a rap at the door.

"Anyone home?" Jase called.

"Come on in. We're baking our bedtime snack."

The aroma of freshly baked chocolate chip cookies filled the small cottage as Jase came in and sniffed appreciatively. "I thought I smelled cookies when I was walking over here. If he gets a whiff, you'll soon have Liam here, too."

"That's fine. I haven't met him yet," Sara said as she put a tray of cookies in the oven. She patted Amy on the head. "That's the last tray. Can you get ready for bed now?"

Amy nodded, smiled shyly at Jase and ran into her room.

"You'll have a chance to meet Liam Saturday night," Jase assured her. "That's one of the reasons I came over."

He pushed a small envelope across the counter. "That's your official invitation. There will be increased security around and you'll need to have that with you."

"Do you get many gate-crashers?" she joked.

"You'd be surprised. Once in a while a celebrity shows up and we'll have a tourist or some paparazzi try to get in to take a look. My father guards his privacy and he knows others do, too."

"Do you guard yours?"

"Usually."

Sara pointed to the baked cookies cooling on a rack. "Interested?"

"Sure am," he said with a look that made Sara wonder if he was interested in *her,* too. If he was handing her an invitation to the Raintree Soiree, they weren't having a date. She was simply attending a party thrown at his house. That settled that question.

"Speaking of privacy, there's something I'd like to discuss with you," Jase said.

Amy ran in, her pink Disney-princess nightgown swirling around her. "Cookie time?"

Jase took a cookie from the rack and offered it to her. "My guess is that you're going to need milk to go along with that."

"Three milks, coming up!" Sara wondered why Jase would want to talk to her about privacy. She'd soon know.

After cookies and milk all around, Sara said to Jase, "It's past Amy's bedtime. Do you mind if I put her to bed before we talk?"

"Can Jase read me a story?" Amy asked.

"Oh, I don't know, honey, he might not want to."

But Jase seemed to be considering her daughter's request. "I can read you a story. What's your favorite one?"

Amy took his hand and with her cookie in the other,

pulled him toward her bedroom, chattering about the books
she liked most. Sara didn't know how she felt about Jase
being part of the bedtime ritual. Conrad had never chosen to take part in it. He was either working late at the
store or at his home computer and that had always caused
such mixed feelings inside her. On one hand, she admired
him working so hard to give them a good life. But on the
other…had she chosen a man who wouldn't put father-
hood first? For her, putting Amy to bed was one of the
best parts of motherhood.

The buzzer rang on the stove and she called to Jase
and Amy, "I have to take the cookies out. I'll be right in."

A few minutes later, Sara stopped in the doorway to
Amy's room. Both Amy and Jase were sitting on her single bed. Jase hardly fit, propped against the headboard
with his long legs stretched out in front of him. Amy sat
close to him, engrossed in his reading of *Clifford, the Big
Red Dog.* The book was one of her favorites and Sara was
mesmerized by the sound of Jase's voice, too, as he put
expression into the words and let Amy study the picture
on each page.

Whether he wanted to believe it or not, Jase Cramer was
daddy material. He was so good with kids. Yet a distant
father and unfaithful fiancée made him doubt his ability to
be part of a family. Certainly that double combination was
enough of an impediment, but Sara had the feeling there
was something else Jase wasn't telling her. Something
more. What had happened to him in his childhood before
he'd come to live with Ethan? Did he ever talk about that?

Amy's room always made Sara smile. Even though
they hadn't lived here that long, it was pure little girl. The
pink-and-white gingham spread and curtains reflected
Amy's bright personality. Her colorful toys were stacked
on shelves along the closet wall. There was also a blue egg

crate, specifically for the doll someone had donated and the clothes that fit her. Moppy, the stuffed dog that Jase had given Amy, was already tucked under her daughter's arm as she sat beside him on the bed.

In some ways, Jase looked out of place here. He was so masculine in a girlie-girl room. But in other ways, specifically the way he related to her daughter, he absolutely fit in.

Jase looked up and saw her standing there. There was a flicker of something in his eyes. Sara wasn't sure what that was about. In so many ways, he was a mystery to her. Knowing about a person didn't mean knowing a person. How well she understood that…how well Conrad had taught her that.

Entering the room, Sara perched on the rocker on Amy's side of the bed until Jase finished the story.

When he closed the book, Amy reached over and hugged him. "You read good."

He was tentative at first, and then he hugged her back. "You listen good." Easing off the bed, he stood and set the book on the nightstand. Then he laid his hand on Amy's head and pulled a pink ribbon from under her earlobe. "Look what I found," he said. "You can tie this in your hair and look as pretty as your mom."

Amy wrapped the ribbon around her finger, smiled up at Jase as if he'd given her a precious gift and scooted down on her back in the bed. "Look, Mommy, a pretty ribbon."

"I see. Here, let me put it on your dresser. I'll tie it in your hair tomorrow."

Jase's gaze went from mother to daughter, then back to Sara. "I'll wait in the living room."

"I won't be long."

And she wasn't, because Amy's eyes were almost closed by the time she said her prayers and Sara kissed her goodnight. She left a hot air balloon nightlight burning and closed the door about halfway, remembering all too well the other night and what had happened on the sofa. Whenever she walked into that living room now, she remembered the feel of Jase's hand on her skin, the firmness of his lips on hers, the demanding hunger that she'd been so tempted to meet.

They'd stick to chocolate chip cookies if they were hungry tonight.

Stopping in the kitchen, she put a few on a plate and brought them over to the coffee table. "If you'd like more, feel free. I packaged the first batch up for Marissa. If your dad would like some, I could send a few over for him."

"They're excellent. He actually might like a few."

"Okay, just let me get some tinfoil—"

Jase caught her wrist. "Come here a minute first. I have something I want to tell you and something I want to ask you."

His grip was firm but gentle, too, and she didn't get the feeling that this was anything too serious. She was hypervigilant these days, her antennae always quivering with awareness, just waiting for the next crisis or problem. If she and Amy just had a little bit of a break from disaster, they might get their optimism back again. Amy sure seemed as though *she* was on the road to happiness.

From his jeans pocket Jase pulled a sheet of paper that had been folded into quarters. He unfolded it, smoothed it out. "I would have emailed this to you, but I know you lost your computer in the fire."

"And I don't have a smartphone. I just wanted basic charges."

He nodded as if he understood, then handed her the article. "This is my first article on The Mommy Club—who they are, how they help parents. I've also covered the food drive and summer lunch program, giving contact numbers if anyone wants to help or needs help. Just tell me what you think. Be honest."

She could see he was serious about the honesty part. Did he feel rusty? Had writer's block plagued him the past couple of years? Had everything he'd seen and experienced locked up his heart until he couldn't open it to let it pour onto paper?

As she read the article, she was sitting only a few inches from him on the sofa. When he took a cookie from the coffee table, his leg brushed hers. She didn't move away. She also didn't think he felt the nonchalance he was trying to show her. This article mattered, not only to him, but to the community at large. She knew how important it was.

When she'd finished, she set the article on her lap.

"Well?"

"You're a smooth, professional writer, and you know how to make a story come alive."

"I used to."

"And there was a reason you used to. You whittled down a story to one, two or three children and you told us all about them. You made us care about them. That was always the strength of everything you wrote."

"And now?" he prompted.

"Now, I think this is a great first piece, but it would be even better if you spotlighted someone The Mommy Club had helped."

"Like you?"

That hadn't been at all what she was thinking when she suggested it, and she said quickly, "Oh, no. I don't want to go public. The news story was bad enough."

"I talked to two other women who essentially told me the same thing. So finding that specific story, and going into detail, isn't going to be that easy if no one will cooperate with me."

"But you're such a good persuader."

"Then let me persuade you."

"Jase—"

"I want you to think about it, Sara. I only have to go as far as you want me to go. We can make the article about you moving in here, how grateful you are to have a place to stay, how Amy seems to be her old self again, how you're making new friends. It can be a positive story. That's the point. My details don't have to have anything to do with your marriage, or your debts, or the insurance investigation. That's not the focus of these articles. The point of the articles is to show the community supporting its residents."

"I need to think about it."

"That's fine. Think about it. I'm going to drop this off tomorrow and I'll have a week until the next one's due."

"And if I say no?"

After a long, studying look that made her feel totally self-conscious, he said, "If you won't do it, I'll find someone who will. Kaitlyn can give me a few more names of women to talk to, but I really think your story is the epitome of what The Mommy Club is about."

"Because it's sensational," she said with a sigh.

"Not just sensational. It showed an immediate need that The Mommy Club met. That's what I'd like to focus on. But I won't pressure you."

Just gazing at Jase created a wellspring of pressure inside of her, desire begging to be released. So she concentrated on something else. "Speaking of pressure, did you feel pressured when Amy asked you to read her a story? She doesn't like the word *no,* but she understands it. When she looks up at me with those big brown eyes, I know she's going to be a heartbreaker."

"Reading a story was no big deal."

"It was to her."

He cocked his head and studied her again. "Would you have preferred if I had said no?"

There was a hint of defensiveness in his voice, but curiosity, too.

"Amy has never had a male role model except for Conrad."

"Was he a good dad?"

"I don't think she remembers him. He didn't interact with her very much. Maybe because he was older." After a pause, she was honest with both of them. "No, that wasn't the reason. I just don't think he was a man who enjoyed being around kids. He didn't like to get down on the floor, on her level. It was hard for him to play silly games. But she was used to him being around, and after he died, there was a hole in her life." She shrugged. "I haven't dated, Jase. I haven't brought any men home."

He understood exactly what she was trying to say. "You're afraid she'll get attached to me."

"She doesn't ask just *anybody* to read her a story."

His voice turned tender when he said, "You're a good mom, Sara."

"I just try to protect her. I don't want to see her get hurt."

He reached out to her and ran his index finger slowly across her lip. "And *you* don't want to get hurt, either."

The tip of his finger was rough and sensual. Her lip felt on fire and that fire was rushing to other parts of her body. How could one little touch make her feel so restless and excited and hungry? Still, she pulled her thoughts together and turned the question around on him.

"Do you?"

He looked as if getting hurt again wouldn't happen if he didn't want it to. "I don't get hurt easily anymore."

"Is that because you don't jump in…because you keep walls up?"

"You don't pull punches."

"I can't."

"Yes, you can. You can have a little fun without bringing Amy into this."

"So you're interested in fun?"

"I don't have the answers to your questions, Sara. I just know there's an attraction between us I haven't felt in a very long time."

*A very long time.* Since his fiancée? That was a question she didn't ask because she knew the answer. Ever since he'd come home, Jase had walled himself off from loving and caring, either in a man-woman relationship or with his father. She didn't have to be a therapist to see that. So what were the chances he could become vulnerable with her? What were the chances *she* could become vulnerable with him?

"I don't compartmentalize very well," she admitted.

"Maybe not. But some day your needs as a woman could break out over your need to protect Amy."

"That won't happen."

He gave her a look that told her *she* was in denial, too. Then he backed off and changed the topic. "Think about the article," he said.

Sara switched gears to follow him. "Did you ask Marissa?"

"I did and she said no."

"Probably for the same reasons I did."

"Kaitlyn's thinking about it. I'd really like to get her interview since she's one of the main organizers of The Mommy Club. I'd like to get yours because the fire's already news."

"Oh, Jase, I—"

"No more pressure," he said, holding his hands up. "I promise. I'll respect your decision either way. But just think about how getting your story out will help other parents. Isn't that the best way to show your gratitude?"

He was good…and even somewhat convincing in more matters than just the article. But she wasn't going to do anything impulsive or reckless. She just wasn't.

The next day, Sara treated her last client of the morning—a microbiologist with neck and shoulder tightness due to too much time spent at his microscope—with the certain knowledge she could help the man manage his profession and his recovery if he was willing to make a few changes. Change was so hard for anyone, including her. Could she change her thinking about becoming involved with a man again to explore her attraction to Jase? The soiree might be the first step.

Before she could attend the party, she had to find something to wear. She realized she might not be able to find anything in the half hour she had at lunchtime. However, she was going to try. Marissa had seemed confident she'd find a dressy dress at Thrifty Solutions. But when Sara thought about the winery and the main house and Ethan and Jase, she knew she needed something classy and maybe even a little spectacular.

Knowing the odds of that, she decided to settle on the classic little black dress. That would have to do.

Thrifty Solutions sported a green awning with green-and-white trim. The window display was attractive, with both men's and women's apparel. When Sara entered, she was surprised at the amount of racks and clothing. Lots of residents must donate and that made her feel good. Ever since the fire, she'd realized Fawn Grove was a giving community, and she and Amy were a part of that.

To her surprise, she saw Kaitlyn at the counter at the cash register. "Hi there! I didn't expect to see you here."

She had called Kaitlyn yesterday to ask about babysitters. Kaitlyn said Marissa had already been in touch and she'd be glad to watch Amy and Jordan for the evening.

"Thursday's my day off. After hospital rounds, I volunteer here for a few hours. Are you looking for something special?"

"A dress for Saturday night. I'll check the racks for something simple and black."

Kaitlyn studied her with an eagle eye.

"What?" Sara asked.

"I might have just the thing. I started unpacking boxes in the back and I saw some dresses you might like. Can you watch over things out here while I look?"

"Sure, no problem."

Kaitlyn wasn't gone long and no one came in or out of the store while she was absent. Sara had drifted from here to there, thinking she really should pick up some tops for Amy.

When Kaitlyn returned, Sara had to blink twice. She was holding a color-blocked black-and-white sheath with glass beads stitched along the bodice and around the checkerboard hem. In her other hand a flaming red dress dangled on a hanger. Both were eye-catching and beautiful.

"I wouldn't expect something like those to be here."

Kaitlyn laughed. "We get everything from sandals to ostrich feather hats. But these… We have a donor who lives in Sacramento. Actually, I think she goes out and buys some of these dresses and donates them. I received a note from her last year in one of the boxes that said, 'Everyone should feel pretty.' So here's your chance. I think they're your size. Why don't you go in the back and try them on."

Sara checked her watch. She had about fifteen minutes. She could do it.

In the back, amidst cartons and racks, price tags, shoes,

shirts and jeans, she quickly slipped out of her scrubs and into the red dress. With plunging décolletage, it just wasn't *her*. She hung it on a waiting rack. She tried to find tags after she slipped out of it, but they had been snipped out. She slipped on the black-and-white sheath. Immediately she felt like a celebrity. She didn't think she'd ever had on a dress that felt so sumptuous.

She went to the doorway of the shop and smiled at Kaitlyn, holding her arms out.

"What do you think?" she asked.

"I think it's perfect for you, and it's perfect for the party."

"Have you ever been to the soiree?"

"A few years ago. My life was entirely different then."

She didn't say any more and again Sara wondered what her story was, and why she was so involved with The Mommy Club. But one thing she'd learned in her practice was a respect for other people's privacy. She usually knew when to poke and when to keep silent. Whatever the reason, this seemed to be a time to keep silent.

"How much is it?" Sara asked, now worried that she couldn't afford it, even if it was in a thrift shop.

"That box had a label on it. Everything in it was supposed to be ten dollars."

"You *are* kidding."

"This is why we have benefactors. Take it, Sara, and enjoy it."

Hours later, at the Fawn Grove Physical Therapy Center, Sara was setting aside case notes on her last patient of the day. She'd seen Ramona twice now and her heart went out to her. The woman had been bicycling when a car's tire blew and the vehicle hit her. Sara still couldn't believe the condition the woman was in. With a pin in her leg and a long scar across her cheek, she was still weak. Sara was working on helping her strengthen her whole body while her leg healed. She helped her work her good leg on the table mat, use hand weights to build up the muscles in her arms again. They also worked on stretching Ramona's neck muscles and loosening her back muscles.

After their first session, Sara realized that Ramona didn't know if she could get better. She wanted her old life back—leading trail rides into the mountains, going out on dates with men who thought she was pretty, having enough energy to keep her going all day and into the night. In some ways, Ramona reminded Sara of Jase when he'd first come home. She just hoped she could help her turn her attitude around, too.

How to do it was the dilemma.

"How many weeks until I'm not so tired?" Ramona asked.

Intuitively, Sara knew Ramona's fatigue came from her mindset as well as her physical condition. "Are you walking at home?"

"Some. But I hate using a cane."

"As soon as you feel you have your balance steady without it, you can carry it instead of use it. Soon you'll be leaving it behind."

Ramona gave her a look that said she didn't believe that would happen anytime soon.

After work, Sara picked up Jordan and Amy and headed back to the winery. Jordan babbled to Amy in the backseat of the car. Marissa's one-year-old had a sunny disposition and a smile that could charm the clouds from the sky.

A short time later, holding Amy's hand and carrying Jordan, Sara walked into the winery's office, looking forward to dinner with Amy, a game or two and then an early bedtime for both of them.

Marissa must have seen her fatigue because she asked, "Are you as beat as you look?"

Sara laughed. "I probably look worse than I feel. I had a tough client this afternoon and I'm not sure what's the best thing to do for her."

"Why don't you take a walk? I'll take Jordan and Amy out to the back garden. They can watch the butterflies. The fountain's going and Jordan loves to splash in the water. Do you mind if Amy gets wet?"

"Not at all. But you've had a long day, too."

"Yeah, but mine was mostly about pushing papers."

One thing Sara had learned through all of this was to accept help graciously. So without further argument, she simply said, "Thanks," and after a kiss and hug for her daughter, headed out the way she'd come in.

She had glimpsed the garden in the back of the office building. There were also gardens surrounding the winery where patrons could sit and enjoy small pastries and salted snacks with the varieties of wine. But she headed in the other direction toward the vineyard, passing a rose garden that was lush with scent and color. She dawdled there for a few minutes, running her finger over the beautifully smooth petals, sniffing the raspberry-scented red roses. In a way, the vineyard and gardens seemed to come from a fairy tale. They were all well cared for and beautiful. She could see why this place had helped Jase heal.

She was strolling through the Merlot vineyard before she knew it. Suddenly Sara saw movement ahead, near one of the trellises. It was Jase, but he wasn't training and tying vines today. He had a camera in his hand. Cautiously, she took a few steps closer. She didn't know whether she should alert him to her presence or not. He said he hadn't used a camera since he'd been home. She didn't want to spoil the moment.

However, as she studied him, she realized he seemed to be shooting panoramic shots, rounding in a circle to capture every aspect of the vineyard. When he trained the camera in her direction, he, of course, saw her.

As he approached her, she automatically said, "If you want to be alone, I can head on back."

"No need for that." His gaze took in her blue scrubs and her brightly colored blouse. Her work uniform, such as it was.

"Are you just home from work?" he asked her.

"I picked up Jordan and Amy, and Marissa's showing them the back garden. She thought I looked like I needed to clear my head."

"Rough day?"

Sometimes she couldn't tell if Jase was just making conversation or if he really wanted to know. He had an easy way of listening that sometimes confused her. She didn't know if he was personally interested in her or practicing his skill as a good photojournalist and reporter.

"The afternoon was. Actually, my patient brought back memories of you when you were recovering. She's having a tough time changing her life."

"Ah, change, the constant in our lives," he said with a wry smile.

Venturing a little closer to him, she motioned to his camera. "What are you up to?"

"Photographs for the new brochure for the vineyard. My father hasn't revitalized it in a few years, so I suggested we do that. We've made some changes in the tasting room, and in the party reception hall. The Wine Club is growing and we need new material."

It seemed as if he was enjoying what he was doing. But she asked the obvious question. "How does it feel to have a camera in your hands again?"

When his gaze locked on hers, she felt the thrill she'd been feeling ever since she moved onto Raintree Winery and encountered him. The sensations that coursed through her whenever she looked into his eyes were almost body-rocking.

"Actually, it feels damn good! I didn't realize how much I'd missed it. I thought when I picked up my camera, memories would come rushing back, the memories I didn't want to revisit. Sure, I remember the last time I was taking pictures and what happened that day, but I also remember roaming these vineyards as a teenager with a camera in my hand. This place is what got me started photographing in the first place, and my camera is what got me name recognition and a byline. When I wrote that article about The Mommy Club, it felt natural, and holding this again does, too." He held up his camera.

"Natural enough that you'll leave again?"

She kept her voice light as if the answer was of no consequence to her.

"We'll see. I accept change a little more readily now than I used to."

Did he really? Would he seek out editors who could use his skills once more?

That thought pushed her heart practically to her knees. She realized whether she wanted to get involved with Jase Cramer or not, she was falling for him. That thought was as terrifying as the possibility that the insurance claim might not go through, and all she'd have left was her job—and a mountain of debt.

Yet that wasn't true. Most of all, she had Amy. Whether she was falling for Jase or not simply didn't matter.

Because Amy came first.

## Chapter Six

"Thank goodness for Kaitlyn." Late Saturday afternoon at her apartment in town, Marissa used the curling iron one last time to put the finishing touches on Sara's new hairdo.

She'd convinced Sara that she needed a little trim for tonight's party. Kaitlyn had come over to the cottage midafternoon to care for Jordan and Amy, and they'd gone to Marissa's for a few hours of party preparation.

Zeroing in on what Marissa had said, Sara was grateful, too, to have this bit of time for girl talk with a woman who was fast becoming a good friend.

Marissa's apartment was small but neat and clean, with charming touches that made it homey. Sara still didn't really know much about her.

"I love Jordan dearly," Marissa went on, "but sometimes it's nice to remember who I was before he was born. Do you know what I mean?"

Since Sara knew all the responsibilities of being a single mom, she definitely understood. "I know what you mean, and I guess I'm finally learning to accept some help, like you are."

"You mean The Mommy Club? I don't know what I would have done without them. I don't know what I would have done without Kaitlyn. When my momma died, I felt lost, really adrift. I think that's why I hooked up with Jordan's father. My mother would have warned me against getting involved with a cowboy, a bull rider, no less."

"So he's not around?"

"Definitely not. He's out on the circuit, doing his thing."

"So he never sees Jordan?"

"He doesn't *know* about Jordan."

That shocked Sara, and Marissa must have glimpsed that look in her eyes when she dipped down in front of Sara to check the curls around her face. "Believe me," Marissa said, "he wouldn't want to know. He wouldn't know responsibility if it bit him. I did the best thing for both of us by not telling him."

Marissa took a mirror from her kitchen table and held it up for Sara to see. "What do you think?"

Marissa had piled Sara's hair on top of her head and made all kinds of swirly curls. A few dangled around her face.

"It looks fabulous!"

"It will look even better once you add that dress. It's a good thing we wear the same size shoes so you can borrow my silver heels."

"Are you sure you don't want to wear them?"

"Nope, my dress is green. I have cream strappy sandals that will look good with it. The silver ones are left over from my kick-up-my-heels days."

Sara had to laugh at the way Marissa said it. "You sound

as if you're never going to have kick-up-your-heels days again."

"I know better now. I'd never go out with someone like Ty again. Oops! I usually don't mention his name. I really don't want anyone to know who Jordan's father is. That way, there's no slip."

"Your secret's safe with me. This isn't Ty Conroy you're talking about, is it?" Ever since she'd lived in Fawn Grove, she'd heard about Ty Conroy, the championships and purses he'd won, the risks he'd taken, the bulls he'd ridden. In a cowboy sense, he was one of those hometown heroes. He'd made good and that was important.

"I won't confirm or deny. That way, you don't really know for sure."

Obviously she wasn't the only one with a trust issue.

"Do you think we should call the kids before we get dressed?" Sara asked.

Marissa pulled a pitcher of iced tea from the refrigerator. "Of course we should. We won't have any peace of mind unless we do. We're moms."

An hour and a half later, Sara and Marissa walked up the front steps of Raintree Winery's main house. Sara didn't feel like herself at all. Yes, she'd gone to cocktail parties with Conrad. But for the past two years, parties hadn't been part of her life. And she'd never been to such an elaborate one as this.

As the butler opened the door and motioned her and Marissa inside, Sara felt out of place in the house's grandeur. The foyer was as big as the living room and kitchen at the cottage, with a beautiful Carrara marble floor, thick wooden arches and beautiful crown molding.

"Wow," she said under her breath.

"I second that," Marissa agreed.

The butler motioned them into the dining room, explaining that beyond was the living room where many of the guests were gathered. They should make themselves comfortable.

"Is Jase going to meet you here?" Marissa asked her.

"Oh, no. I mean, this isn't a date or anything. He just invited me to come."

"Once he sees you in that dress, I think he'll want to spend some time with you."

"My dress won't sway the way he thinks, one way or another. He's not that kind of man."

"Believe me, Sara, if he's attracted to you—and I think he is—that dress is going to ratchet up his attraction. So be prepared."

"For what?"

"To have a great time tonight."

"Are you going to desert me?"

"Not exactly. But part of my job is to mingle with the clients, strike up conversations, find out what they like about our wines as well as what they don't. Jase wants me to discover some of that tonight. As general manager, he has to keep on top of it, and talking with the guests invited to this party is the best way to do it."

Marissa patted Sara's arm. "Go on, mingle. I'll be all over the place. You'll find me."

Sara felt completely out of her element, mainly because she'd forgotten how to make small talk at a cocktail party. But maybe like other remembered skills, that one would return when she needed it.

Although the house was big and luxurious, the furnishings called to her. There was an oil painting of the Sierras on one wall. She studied it for a while, wondering if any of Jase's photographs decorated any other walls. In another corner sat an unusual club chair, the fabric printed with photographs of Raintree Winery.

"Distinctive, isn't it?" a tall, blond man with a wine-glass in his hand asked her, his gaze roaming over her as if he was trying to figure out who she was.

"Yes, it is. I was wondering if Jase might have taken the photographs." There was a perspective about the photos that reminded her of some of his pictures.

"You have a good eye, or else you've seen a lot of Jase's work. You a friend of his?"

She automatically extended her hand. "I'm Sara Stevens. My daughter and I are staying in the cottage."

"So *you're* Sara. I finally meet the single mom who escaped the fire. Quite heroic, rescuing your daughter like that."

"Not really. Just something a mother does."

As he shook her hand, his thumb pressed almost intimately along her palm and she quickly pulled her hand away.

But he just smiled a charming smile and introduced himself. "I'm Liam Corbett, chief winemaker. I've seen your car come and go, but I haven't had the pleasure of meeting you."

She relaxed a little, now that she knew who he was. What she'd thought had been a come-on might simply have been Liam being friendly. "You create award-winning wines."

"I try. I was around the block before I came here. Just couldn't find the quite-right grapes, soil, temperature. But Raintree has it all."

In his mid-forties, with his blond good looks, tanned skin and green eyes, Liam could be a lady-killer.

"So your little girl is four?" he asked with a cock of his head and another smile that was meant to disarm her.

She knew that, but his warmth and charm were inviting at a party in the midst of strangers. "Yes, she is. And she's my life." She found herself admitting, "I haven't attended a party like this for a long while."

"Well, then, you have to make the most of the night you have. Come on, let me introduce you to some people."

Why not? Liam was Jase's colleague and seemed genuinely interested in helping her have a good time.

Before, Sara had stood on the fringe of the groups, trying to figure out how she wanted to jump in...*if* she wanted to jump in. But now Liam swept her right to the center of the action. In the living room, he laid his hand on the small of her back and guided her toward a group of men and women. She knew his hand on her back was simply a courtesy, but it didn't feel right. She moved ahead, letting it slip off, but not before she spotted Jase. He'd been watching her and Liam cross the room. Though she tried, she couldn't read his expression and she wondered if *he* would be spending any time with her tonight.

Before she could give the question more thought, Liam introduced her to a round of guests. One was a food writer for the *L.A. Times,* another a chef at a five-star restaurant. After a few minutes of conversation that Liam facilitated, the woman who had accompanied the chef looked Sara over. "Beautiful dress. The designer's Carzanne, isn't it?"

Designer? Sara really hadn't kept up with designers. How could the woman tell? Quickly she said, "The dress just seemed right for tonight."

"That it is. You've got a lot of heads turning. Liam's, of course. But Mr. Cramer's, too. He hasn't taken his eyes off you since you walked in."

Was that true? Had she wowed Jase?

Another couple joined the group and Sara recognized the gentleman. He'd had a sports injury. After arthroscopic surgery, she'd helped him build up his leg muscles again.

However, like any health-care professional, she didn't give away the identity of her clients.

He remembered her, however, and didn't hesitate to say, "Sara! I never expected to see *you* here." He put his arm around his wife. "Margery, this is my physical therapist, the one who got me playing tennis again."

Suddenly a deep baritone over Sara's shoulder said, "She's good at what she does. I should know."

The group went silent for a minute as Jase stepped into their circle. In a tuxedo, pristine white shirt and black tie, he was absolutely magnificent. So much so, that Sara had to swallow hard as she looked at him. His gaze on her was assessing, admiring, maybe even a little intimate. And maybe she was reading way too much into a look…just because of an errant kiss.

Music had begun on the patio outside the French doors in the dining room. There were tables set up there and couples were going out to the patio to dance.

Jase gazed in that direction for a fraction of a second, and then he held his hand out to her. "How about some fresh air and music?"

Sharing music and a dance with Jase sounded wonderful about now, so she nodded. They made their excuses and Jase led her outside to the patio. He headed to one of the corners, slightly in shadow.

Holding her loosely as they danced, he asked, "So what do you think of Raintree's soiree?"

Easily she responded, "I think it's elegant and tasteful, and everyone seems to be enjoying themselves."

"You included?"

There was a hint of something in Jase's tone that told her his question was more than conversational. She wasn't sure exactly what he was asking, but something seemed to be on his mind. "Marissa and I split up when we came in, and I felt out of my element at first."

"That's natural when you don't know anyone. Liam seemed to put you at ease."

She wasn't exactly sure what to say to that. After all, he and Liam worked together. So she said, "Liam's nice. And friendly. He made me feel not so out of place. He introduced himself and then insisted I get to know everyone here."

"I see," Jase said, then added, "Some women find him hard to resist."

"As in plural *women?*"

"When Liam's not making wine, he's an adventurer. He mountain climbs, rock climbs, likes to sample beaches in Croatia and South America."

"You're telling me he's multidimensional," she said lightly, joking, although Jase's tone was serious.

"I'm telling you he likes diversity in his adventures *and* in his women."

She felt as if Jase was warning her away from Liam. For her sake...or his? "I'll keep that in mind." It wasn't as if Jase could advise her on who she should or shouldn't see. It wasn't as if he had any right to say. Not that she'd fall for Liam's practiced charm and easy conversation.

Jase seemed to accept her response for what it was: a declaration of her independence. But then his hand held hers a little tighter and he pulled her just a little closer. "You look beautiful tonight. Any man here would like to spirit you off to his own private beach or vineyard or whatever."

Some imp inside her who'd been sleeping for a while urged her to ask, "Including you?"

He must have taken her question as the flirtation she'd meant it to be because he shifted their hands onto his chest and pulled her even closer. His thighs brushed hers as the music played. "I think I made it obvious that I'd like to do that, but we both know there are consequences."

"To private beaches, not to dancing."

"There, we think alike." He bent his head slightly. As she leaned her face closer to his, his jaw grazed her cheek.

Often Jase had a sexy beard stubble from not shaving that day. But tonight he was clean shaven, smelled spicy and musky and was looking at her as if he wanted to swallow her up. As they moved to the rhythm of the music, Sara forgot where she was and remembered only whom she was with. Their bodies leaned into each other naturally as if it were the best place to be. When Jase's hand played with stray curls at her neck, she trembled.

"You remind me of Cinderella tonight."

"I *will* have to leave before midnight. I don't want to keep Kaitlyn too late, or have Amy miss me too much."

"She'll be asleep."

"Yes, but if she wakes up and I'm not there— I don't want her to ever think I abandoned her."

He nodded as if he understood that. Maybe he did understand even better than she did. His foot brushed against hers. "Don't lose one of those shoes on the way out."

"You like the heels?" she teased.

"Oh, I like the heels," he assured her. "You have great legs and they make that obviously clear."

Jase's compliment sounded genuine and sincere.

"Marissa loaned me the shoes," she said, then admitted, "I do feel a little like Cinderella tonight."

When she tipped her face up to his, Jase was glancing over the guests gathered on the patio. He wrapped his arm around her waist and guided her down the step into one of the gardens. There was an arbor there with climbing roses, shadows and all the sweet scents of summer mingling into a lovely night. It provided privacy and she found she was glad for it. Everything about tonight felt a little dreamlike, including being here with Jase like this. Was he experiencing the same feelings?

He seemed to answer her unspoken question when he said, "I'm glad you came tonight."

"Did you think I wouldn't?"

"I thought you might back out at the last minute."

"Marissa wouldn't let me."

"Good for Marissa." His voice was husky as he again fingered one of the curls dangling along her cheek.

A little nervous, she murmured, "You have responsibilities here tonight."

"Not at the moment," he assured her. He hesitated a moment, then confessed, "Ever since we kissed, I've been imagining kissing you again."

He knew she was skittish about getting involved with a man again and he wasn't pushing. But he was leading her into new territory that both scared and excited her. Talking about their kiss made the idea of doing it again even more tempting.

"I've thought about it a lot. I know neither of us wants to get hurt. I particularly understand that neither of us will find trusting someone easy or simple."

"But?" she asked shakily.

His thumb slowly traced her lower lip. "But…there's a bond between us and an attraction that for me began two years ago. The question is—Do I want to fight it? Do you?"

Everything he was saying was so true. And yet tonight, with these Cinderella-type feelings bubbling up inside her, she *didn't* want to fight them.

So she simply said, "I'd like you to kiss me again."

As he circled her with his arms and brought her close, she reached up around his neck. Jase's kiss had the ability to make her forget who she was as well as where she was. Music from the patio wafted around them as his lips sensually moved over hers, as his kiss intoxicated her more than any of the Raintree wines. When his tongue coaxed her lips apart, she remembered his taste and the masculine possessiveness that characterized the way he kissed. Conrad's kisses had satisfied them both, but Jase's kisses promised so much more…filled her with a sense of joy… heated her through and through.

As Jase groaned, angled his mouth, took the kiss deeper, she realized he felt the same way.

A kiss was *not* just a kiss. Not ever. Not when there was this much passion and desire behind it. Not when there was this much hunger left to be satisfied.

Sara found herself seeking Jase's heat, not just in the kiss, but elsewhere. She lowered her hands from his neck, reached inside his open tux jacket, exploring the leanness of his waist and then the breadth of his back.

Jase broke away and whispered huskily, "Sara, if you keep that up, I'm going to roll that zipper down the back of your dress."

When she froze, he trailed kisses down her neck and then shook his head. "I like it. A lot. But I think we're going to have to cool this down if we don't want to end up naked under the arbor where the guests might come strolling by at any minute."

*Was* kissing Jase a mistake if she could get lost so easily?

Jase must have known exactly where her thoughts were heading because he cupped her face in his hands and looked deep into her eyes. "Don't tell me that was a mistake. Each kiss just tells me that we both want the same thing."

"What? A fling under a rose arbor?"

He studied her thoughtfully. "That's what we're going to have to decide. But not at this moment. Come on. Why don't I show you the wine cellar?"

"More private than the arbor?" she asked, confused and uncertain where her life was headed.

"Not tonight. The wine cellar's open for our guests to see. They can come and go from the party, so most likely we'll have company."

"A good thing," she murmured…and he laughed.

Jase didn't guide Sara inside the house. Rather they took a path aglow with foot lamps and ended up on a level below the first floor in front of a solid wood door.

"This is usually locked. But tonight we're keeping it open. Hopefully our guests won't steal the most expensive wines."

The door creaked as he opened it and they stepped inside. Right away Sara could see this private wine cellar was an amazing space. Exposed beams ran across the ceiling. The walls were gray stone. There were tilted racks upon tilted racks of wine bottles. The temperature was cool but not unpleasantly so, maybe because she'd been so hot after that kiss. As they toured from the end of one row to another, Jase pulled bottles of different kinds of wines, showing her their dates, explaining their value. When they came to the end of a row, Sara heard a babble of voices.

Jase just gave a shrug. "Everyone wants to see what Dad keeps down here."

That was the first time she'd heard Jase call Ethan *Dad*. Was it a slip? Maybe he was just afraid to let his fondness for the man show. She wondered if Ethan's crusty exterior went deeper than that. Was he crusty all the way to his heart? Or was there some marshmallow in there, too? Most people weren't one extreme or the other, and she'd learned from dealing with all of her patients that most had walls they were afraid to let crumble.

As the group approached their row, Jase mumbled, "I guess my father's giving this tour himself."

She soon recognized Ethan's voice as he explained the layout of the wine cellar. As soon as he turned into their row, he stopped. "I see someone else is taking the tour."

There was forced joviality in his voice, and Sara knew that was because of her. Was he afraid she'd take Jase away from Raintree? Or was he really afraid she was a manipulative woman who just wanted to share in his son's success and wealth?

There were three couples with Ethan. As introductions were made and everyone shook hands, Sara realized she'd seen some of them milling about upstairs earlier.

As the men discussed vintages, Mrs. Campbell, the wife of a man who was CEO of a tech company, sidled up to her. "I love your dress. That's a Carzanne, isn't it?"

When she'd migrated around cocktail parties with Conrad, sure, she'd noticed pretty dresses. But she hadn't known what designers did what. What *was* it about her dress that made it so recognizable?

Mrs. Campbell answered that question for her. "Carzanne usually does the color blocking with the beading across the bodice and checkerboard hem."

What could Sara say? The tags had been cut out when she'd found the dress at the thrift shop. She simply said, "Every designer's work is distinctive in some way."

When she glanced toward Ethan, she saw he'd been listening to their conversation.

"Why don't we all head upstairs," Ethan said, including Jase and Sara. "The caterer refilled the food trays. Wine is flowing, and Liam and Tony are going to give a short presentation about all our newest varieties. I wouldn't want you to miss that."

"I'll be along in a few minutes," Jase said to his father.

Ethan didn't look as if he approved, but he graciously escorted his guests through another door and up the stairs.

"He obviously wants you to go along," Sara said.

"He obviously knows I'd rather spend time with you."

She liked the idea of spending time with Jase. Still, she insisted, "I don't want to come between you."

"There are a lot of things between my father and me. You're not one of them."

She heard the sadness in Jase's voice and wished she could do something about it. "I really should find Marissa. We made a pact not to stay too late. We don't want to take advantage of Kaitlyn. She's used to kids in her practice, but handling a four-year-old and a one-year-old for hours at a time could be a bit wearing."

There was a look in Jase's eyes that said he wanted to kiss her again. Instead, however, he held out his arm. "Come on, I'll escort you upstairs. Maybe I can convince you to have a glass of wine before you leave."

Maybe he could.

"I heard what Lisa Campbell said. She noticed that dress Sara Stevens was wearing was a Carzanne! He dresses stars on the red carpet." Jase's father had confronted him as soon as everyone had left around midnight.

After Jase loosened his tie, he yanked it off. "I'm sure Sara didn't purchase a Carzanne from the designer. The Mommy Club has been helping her, and my guess is that someone loaned her the dress."

"Then why didn't she say that when asked about it?"

"Would you have told someone you were wearing a borrowed suit?"

His father seemed to think about that, then grudgingly admitted, "Maybe not."

"Marissa loaned her the shoes."

"You know this how?"

"Sara told me. I made some comment about Cinderella." Ethan gave him an odd look.

"What?" Jase asked.

"Nothing. I just don't like where you seem to be headed."

"You said the same thing when I began traveling from one refugee camp to another. Look how that turned out. I won a Pulitzer." As soon as Jase said it, he knew he shouldn't have.

"You also almost lost your life."

His father's voice held a trace of something Jase hadn't heard there before, not even when he'd been flown back here from Africa and ended up in a hospital in L.A. His father had been waiting there when Jase had been wheeled in. Back then, he'd been efficient, talking to doctors, making sure Jase had the best care. He'd wanted his son to stay there for in-house rehabilitation. Jase had wanted to be at Raintree again, smell the scent of ripening grapes, feel the cool night air, hear the birds sing.

Thank goodness he'd come back, because he'd met Sara and she'd helped him put his world back on its axis.

In a way, however, so had his father.

Changing the subject, Ethan untied his own tie and let it hang around his neck. "You're doing a fine job as general manager of Raintree. You know that, don't you?"

"Profits are up, distribution channels are opening wider and the wine club is growing. So, yes, I can see progress." He remembered how he'd savored praise from his father in his first years after he'd arrived here. That praise had always seemed to center around work on the vineyard. Ethan appreciated anything that made it thrive.

"Liam has added more life to the wines, too. He's inventive." Jase had to give the man his due.

"You were watching him closely tonight. Were you concerned he'd make a pass at one of our married clients?"

"You never know with Liam."

What Jase had been watching for was Liam putting the moves on Sara. Jealousy gnawed at him at the thought. He had no right to *be* jealous. Yet Sara had seemed comfortable with Liam when they were talking. An instant connection?

Shedding his tux jacket, Jase tossed it over a chair. "I'm going for a walk."

"Toward the cottage?" His father wanted to know.

Jase tossed him a look that told him it was none of his business.

## Chapter Seven

Yes, he'd taken a walk toward the cottage. It seemed he and Sara always had something to settle. Or was he just making excuses to see her, to kiss her again?

More than likely, she would have already turned in.

Jase's pulse raced a little faster as he spotted a light burning in her living room. Insomnia? Worry about her and Amy's future? Or racing thoughts like the ones scrambling in his mind for dominance?

He opened the screen door and rapped lightly. After all, she might have simply forgotten to switch off the lamp.

Within a minute or so, the outside light came on and her door opened. She obviously hadn't been in bed, but... she was *dressed* for bed.

The innocent-looking yellow cotton gown and robe could have been sedate on any woman, but on Sara—

His heart sped up a little more.

To her credit, she didn't ask why he was there. They

were drawn to each other and fighting the chemistry magnet. But she did tie the belt on her robe a little tighter. An indication her guard was up and she wouldn't be giving in to desire?

"Did everyone leave?" she asked.

Although the porch lamp glowed, most of her face was still in shadow.

"Even the catering staff."

"It was a nice party."

Most people wouldn't consider her term accurate. "Nice?"

"All right," she admitted with a smile in her voice. "It was glamorous."

"That had to do with the caliber of guests. Can I come in?"

She seemed wary. "To talk about the party?"

"Among other subjects."

"It's late."

"It's the weekend."

After a pensive pause, she stepped back and let him in.

He'd removed his cuff links and rolled up his shirt-sleeves. With his shirt collar opened, he thought a more casual appearance might put her at ease. As he crossed her threshold, she eyed him as if his more casual look didn't relax her at all.

He waited for her to make the next move. Should he stand there and talk? Sit on the sofa? Head to the kitchen table?

For a moment, she didn't react. She just let her gaze roam from his open shirt collar to his rolled up sleeves. She bit on her lower lip and he almost reached out and pulled her into his arms.

Almost.

"Can we sit?" he suggested before he did something stupid. He was well aware Amy was in a room close by.

Sara went to the sofa and curled up against the arm, her legs—long, very curvy legs—tucked beneath her.

Lowering himself to the middle cushion, he asked, "Did everything go okay with Amy, Jordan and Kaitlyn?"

"Kaitlyn knows her way around children. They were both sleeping when Marissa and I came in. I think Kaitlyn tired them out, which is a real feat. Even Marissa was impressed because Jordan didn't wake up when she put him in her car."

He had trouble taking his eyes from Sara. Her hair was still a mass of curls on top of her head and those stray ones around her face were driving him crazy. "You looked beautiful tonight. I liked your hair that way."

"It only took an hour and Marissa's patience, so once I take it down, you might never see this side of me again."

She said it lightly but he could tell she was serious.

"You made an impact. More than one guest commented on your dress."

"So you overheard," Sara murmured and a defiant look entered her eyes. "And I suppose your father did, too. You both think I went online with a computer that hasn't been replaced yet and bought a dress from Luca Carzanne with thousands of dollars I don't have!"

She'd almost risen from the sofa—he was sure she was ready to show him the door—when he clasped her arm to stop her. "Sara."

Whether it was the timbre of his voice or the firmness of his clasp or the directness of his gaze, he wasn't sure. But she went still and just stared at him.

"Yes, my father overheard and commented. I told him I was sure The Mommy Club had helped you in some way, along with Marissa."

Glancing at her feet, he knew she was thinking about those very high-heeled, sexy shoes.

"I always feel I'm defending myself around you. Do you know how uncomfortable that is?"

When he kept silent, she sighed with resignation. "Your father probably won't believe me, but I found that dress at the thrift shop. Someone donated a box of dressy dresses. Kaitlyn pulled out a couple in my size and that was one of them."

"Why *wouldn't* he believe you?"

"Because he wants to believe the worst about me. He senses…" She stopped, then straightened her shoulders and courageously continued. "He senses you're interested in me. He doesn't want you to get hurt again."

Jase agreed that for some reason his father didn't want him to get involved with Sara, but the rest of her conclusion didn't hold water.

"Your imagination is running away with you. He simply doesn't want anything to interfere with my management of the winery. I don't think he'll approve of my decision to become involved with the newspaper, either, because he wants my focus on Raintree."

"Doesn't he see that your journalism and photography are part of who you are?"

"I wouldn't call that article journalism."

"You don't have to be shot at to write a good story."

That's what he liked about Sara—the bottom line. "You're right. Getting to the heart of an issue is what journalism is about. Or photography, for that matter."

He and Sara connected on so many levels; not the least of them was physical chemistry. As their gazes met and held, he felt the actual ripple of it in the air and the answering response in his body.

Lowering his hand to her bare foot, he playfully ran his

thumb over her arch. "How did your feet hold up in those Cinderella shoes?"

"I think they'd rather run barefoot."

His fingers slid over her arch again, and he massaged until she sighed.

"How did you get so good at that?" she asked. "I'm the one who had massage classes."

"I picked up a few talents in my travels."

Sara was studying him as if she might be imagining other women, other foot massages, but there hadn't been any. Even with Dana. Their affair had been a few weeks here, a quick stopover there. They'd both put their photojournalism careers first, not tender moments to share. But putting all that into words seemed to be too much of a gut-wrenching revelation. Because he understood, now, his relationship with Dana had never been the soul-stirring kind that could be a foundation for a lasting marriage.

When he suspected Sara was going to pull away, he tapped her hot-pink painted toenails. "Couldn't see these with your Cinderella shoes."

Immediately a smile spread across her lips. "Those were Amy's idea. Hers match."

He ran his thumb over her instep and cupped her foot in his hand. The question came out before he could stop it. "Are you afraid of what you feel when you're with me?"

This time when she bit her lower lip, he released her foot and moved closer. "Sara?"

"Your questions are too personal."

"That's why I ask them." He moved nearer still until he was sitting by her hip and she stretched her legs out along the back of the sofa. "Do you want me to leave?"

"You *should* leave."

"That's not what I asked."

She closed her eyes, opened them again and murmured,

"I don't want you to leave. But yes, I am afraid of what I feel when I'm with you."

He leaned in slowly, giving her the chance to move away. But she didn't. And when his lips captured hers, he didn't taste fear but rather desire. The same desire he felt. Questions faded away when they were this close. Physical intimacy seemed to be an answer in itself.

In response to his unspoken question, Sara's arms circled his neck, as his lips took more and demanded more, as arousal became more potent than any of the finest Raintree wines. Yes, Amy was in the next room. No, he wasn't going to go too far. But he was going to go a little further.

Sara's robe had gapped open and he slid his hand inside. The cotton of her gown was simply a soft, pliable barrier that didn't meet any resistance. When he palmed her breast, he felt her answering response vibrate under his hand. Her fingers laced into his hair and she pressed into him, wanting more. He was ready to give it. With as much control as he could muster, he rimmed his finger around her nipple. Now her hand left his hair, circled his back and seemed to be trying to find a place to touch him, skin to skin. There was so much heat between them now that even mountaintop snow couldn't cool him off. She plucked at his shirt and it came loose from the waistband of his trousers. Her hand was underneath it in seconds and he felt her palm on his skin. It felt so good, he could lay her down on the sofa and take her right there and then.

But Amy was in the next room and they both could be sorry in the morning.

The last remaining thought in his head told him what he had to do. He stopped everything…all of it. He moved his hand away from her breast and he stopped kissing her. The moment he put a few inches between them, she looked up at him.

They were both out of breath as if they'd run a race. Maybe they had, but it was a race he couldn't complete this time...not without regrets.

His voice was gravelly when he concluded, "I think a little time and space to think about what we want might be best."

He saw that lift of her chin, the defiant independence that came into her eyes. That was Sara. When she said with forced conviction, "You're right," he wasn't surprised. After all, they were adults with good sense and histories that had made them both cautious.

Turning away from her, trying to get every one of his senses under control along with his libido, he blew out a resigned sigh. Then he stood and said the only thing he could think of to say. "You know where to find me if you need me."

She wouldn't meet his gaze again, and he knew she wasn't going to let him see her need.

So time and space were what he was going to give them...whether they liked it or not.

On Tuesday of the following week, Sara glanced at her watch and then at the clock on the wall at the physical therapy center. She couldn't believe how late it was. Ramona was sitting on one of the table mats, looking forlorn after a grueling workout.

"I just can't count on my leg when I go walking. I have to take my cane along for most of the walk."

"Maybe you're trying to go too far."

"I have to push myself or I'll never get better. You said as much."

"Yes, I did. But you have to know how far to push. Because if you overdo, you'll set yourself back a few steps instead of going forward."

Sara knew Ramona and she needed to discuss this more. The problem was she had to pick up Amy soon.

She patted Ramona's shoulder. "I have to make a call. Rest a few minutes and then we'll talk more about how far to push."

Maybe Marissa could pick up Amy. But trying Marissa's cell, Sara only reached her voice mail. Next she tried the winery.

This time Marissa didn't pick up, but Jase did.

"Raintree Winery, Jase Cramer speaking."

"Jase, I…" She hadn't seen or spoken to him since their sofa session Saturday night. He'd said they needed time and space and she'd most assuredly agreed. "I thought I'd reach Marissa."

"She had the afternoon off today. When she leaves, her calls are forwarded to my line."

"I forgot." Marissa had told her Saturday that she'd be taking a few hours off and Sara needn't pick up Jordan on Tuesday. "I know Kaitlyn probably still has office hours—"

"What's wrong, Sara?"

"I'm tied up with a patient. I was hoping Marissa could pick up Amy at day care today. But I'll figure out something."

"I could pick her up."

She said the first thing that came into her head. "But you don't have a car seat."

"I can easily remedy that. The question is, do you trust me to pick her up and stay with her until you get home?"

Home. The cottage was beginning to feel like home, and that worried her as much as her attraction to Jase. She remembered his walk with Amy, the comfortable way Amy acted around him. "I don't want to take advantage of you. A four-year-old can be a handful, or an armful, or a houseful."

His voice was filled with amusement as he asked, "Are you trying to dissuade me or warn me?"

"Warn you. I just want you to know what you'll be getting into."

"I have been around kids, Sara. I can entertain Amy if that's what you're worried about. I have a key to the cottage. Do you want me to use it? Or would you rather I take her to the house?"

"It would probably be easier for both of you to be at the cottage. I don't mind if you let yourself in."

"Not worried I'll steal the family jewels?"

"There are no jewels."

"That depends on how you look at it."

Was he saying that she and Amy were valuable to him?

"We can see if time and space did either of us any good," he remarked.

"It wasn't much time and space."

"Then why did it seem like it?"

He felt that, too, had he? The sense of loss, the sense of something missing. She had told herself not to look for him in the vineyard, not to watch for his car, but she had anyway and had felt foolish about it.

"I'd better get back to my patient."

"Of course." He sounded as if he understood. "This will work out fine, Sara. Trust me."

The last thing she wanted to do was trust another man. But in this situation, she felt she had no choice.

Over an hour later, Sara laughed out loud when she walked up to the cottage and saw what Jase and her daughter were doing. Were they really playing hopscotch with blue chalk checkerboarded all over the walk?

Amy had just finished hopping in the squares and Jase followed her, hopping, too. He'd been unaware of Sara until she'd started laughing.

Then he looked over his shoulder and grinned at her. "What? You don't think a grown man can play hopscotch?" He was wearing jeans and a T-shirt and sneakers and looked rakish and boyish.

"Sure, a grown man can play hopscotch. After all, I jump rope sometimes. But you totally altered the appearance of the front walk. I don't want your father to think *I* did this."

"I take full responsibility," Jase said seriously. "It's not going to be an issue. This washes off with the hose." He pointed to his camera bag on the small porch. "I took some photos of Amy playing and of her watching the hummingbirds at the feeder. When I get back to my suite, I'll print them out for you."

"I'd love to have them. I lost—" Her voice broke when she thought about losing Amy's precious baby history... over the giving way Jase was recording "now" for her.

Jase could obviously see how she'd choked up. "You lost all your photographs from when Amy was a baby?"

"Yes. Scrapbooks, too. I've been trying to write down what I remembered—about the first time she rolled over, her first tooth, her first steps. You think you'll remember, but sometimes those memories get all mixed up as time slips away."

Jase came over to her and put his arm around her shoulders.

"From this day forward, you can record it all."

"Your photographs today will help. Thank you."

As if Jase was uncomfortable with her gratitude, he dismissed it. "Photos are easy for me. No thanks necessary." Then to put the conversation back on a practical footing, he said, "The insurance investigator must realize you'd never willingly let something important to any parent go."

"I told him about what I lost, but I don't know if it matters to him."

"Well, all of it matters to you. Let's get out that hose, have some fun and take more pictures. Why don't you and Amy change into something you don't mind getting wet."

"What about you?"

"I'm fine."

"I guess that means you think you're going to hold the hose and *not* get wet?"

"I don't like that look in your eye," he teased.

"We're going to have to take turns. That's fair."

"And we do need to be fair."

As they once more made eye contact, the attraction between them was still potent. Though they were fleeting, she remembered each of their kisses. She remembered his touch. Most of all, she remembered that neither of them trusted very well right now...that neither of them wanted to take an emotional risk. But she enjoyed being with him and he seemed to feel the same way about being with her. Tonight they were going to have fun.

Amy ran over to her and Sara stooped down, hugged her and swung her around. "Hi there, Bitsy Bug. How was your day?"

"I played hopscotch with Mr. Jase."

"I can see that. What else did you do?"

"We played froggy. Mr. Jase has a computer."

"It's my tablet," Jase explained. "I downloaded an app for her to play. She seemed to like it."

"Can we get one, Mommy?"

"Not right now, honey. But Jase suggested we wash off the chalk with the hose and play in the water for a while. What do you think? You can play in your swimsuit."

# FREE Merchandise is 'in the Cards' for you!

### Dear Reader,

***We're giving away FREE MERCHANDISE!***

Seriously, we'd like to reward you for reading this novel by giving you **FREE MERCHANDISE** worth over $20. And no purchase is necessary!

You see the Jack of Hearts sticker above? Paste that sticker in the box on the Free Merchandise Voucher inside. Return the Voucher promptly...and we'll send you valuable Free Merchandise!

Thanks again for reading one of our novels—and enjoy your Free Merchandise with our compliments!

*Pam Powers*

Pam Powers

P.S. Look inside to see what Free Merchandise is **"in the cards"** for you!

# FREE MERCHANDISE VOUCHER

2 FREE
BOOKS
and
2 FREE
GIFTS

Please send my Free Merchandise, consisting of
**2 Free Books** and **2 Free Mystery Gifts**.
I understand that I am under no obligation to buy
anything, as explained on the back of this card.

### 235/335 HDL F42P

*Please Print*

|  |
|--|

FIRST NAME

|  |
|--|

LAST NAME

|  |
|--|

ADDRESS

|  |  |
|--|--|

APT.#          CITY

|  |  |
|--|--|

STATE/PROV.     ZIP/POSTAL CODE

## *NO PURCHASE NECESSARY!*

▶ Detach card and mail today. No stamp needed. ▶

© 2013 HARLEQUIN ENTERPRISES LIMITED. ® and ™ are trademarks owned and used by the trademark owner and/or its licensee.

HSE-FM-08/13

**HARLEQUIN**® READER SERVICE—**Here's How It Works:**

Accepting your 2 free books and 2 free gifts (gifts valued at approximately $10.00) places you under no obligation to buy anything. You may keep the books and gifts and return the shipping statement marked "cancel." If you do not cancel, about a month later we'll send you 6 additional books and bill you just $4.74 each in the U.S. or $5.24 each in Canada. That is a savings of at least 14% off the cover price. It's quite a bargain! Shipping and handling is just 50¢ per book in the U.S. and 75¢ per book in Canada.* You may cancel at any time, but if you choose to continue, every month we'll send you 6 more books, which you may either purchase at the discount price or return to us and cancel your subscription.

*Terms and prices subject to change without notice. Prices do not include applicable taxes. Sales tax applicable in N.Y. Canadian residents will be charged applicable taxes. Offer not valid in Quebec. Books received may not be as shown. All orders subject to credit approval. Credit or debit balances in a customer's account(s) may be offset by any other outstanding balance owed by or to the customer. Please allow 4 to 6 weeks for delivery. Offer available while quantities last.

BUSINESS REPLY MAIL
FIRST-CLASS MAIL    PERMIT NO. 717    BUFFALO, NY

POSTAGE WILL BE PAID BY ADDRESSEE

HARLEQUIN READER SERVICE
PO BOX 1867
BUFFALO NY 14240-9952

NO POSTAGE
NECESSARY
IF MAILED
IN THE
UNITED STATES

▲ If offer card is missing write to: Harlequin Reader Service, P.O. Box 1867, Buffalo, NY 14240-1867 or visit www.ReaderService.com ▲

Amy was all for that, so Sara took her inside and they both quickly changed. By the time they returned out front, Jase had attached the hose to the spigot. He showed Amy the nozzle with its fan spray, cone spray and shower spray, and told her to pick one to wash off the blue chalk. She did and the two of them started on one of the squares. Then all of a sudden, Jase shifted the hose so Sara got sprayed. She squealed as the cold water hit her tank top and shorts.

"Just remember, I get a turn," she called to him.

"Oh, I remember." Then he sprayed Amy and she squealed, too. As each blue number and square disappeared, they all got wetter. Jase picked up his camera, snapping photos whenever the hose wasn't aimed at him. When he took control of the water spurts, he would aim the nozzle up in the air and the drizzle would sprinkle down on all of them. The sound of Amy's giggles filled Sara's heart. Jase knew how to play with kids and she loved that fact. He and Amy were coconspirators as they sprayed Sara, but then she grabbed the hose and yanked it out of his hand and turned the tables on him. Pretty soon, he was as wet as they were.

They were all laughing and unaware that someone was watching.

Sara was bent over, her hands on her knees, trying to catch her breath when she spotted the very expensive boots. Her eyes traveled up a pair of creased jeans and a starched snap-button shirt until they landed on Liam's handsome face. She wondered if he'd been at some kind of meeting, or if he always dressed like this around the winery, casually chic.

He winked at her. "Looks as if everyone's having fun."

The wink unsettled her, until she reminded herself that Liam no doubt flirted with any woman in sight. "As much fun as I've had in a long while," she said, knowing it was true.

The hose was lying on the ground and Amy was dancing in and out of it, playing her own little game.

Jase came over to stand beside Sara. "On your way out for the evening?"

"Matter of fact, I am. I just had to see your dad about something first. A friend of mine opened a new restaurant in Sacramento, and I'm driving down there for the night." He held up a hand. "Don't worry. Everything's under control here."

"I don't worry...about your winemaking. You know what you're doing."

"Yes, I do. I like that new brochure that came back from the printer. Marissa's doing a mass mailing, as well as sending them to wine festivals. We should have a good summer." He eyed Jase's wet clothes, then Sara's. "Maybe you should talk to Ethan about putting an inground pool on the property."

"That wouldn't be nearly as much fun," Sara said, not wanting Liam to feel she was ignoring him.

Though she was beginning to feel a little self-conscious standing there in her wet outfit. She hadn't felt self-conscious with Jase, but she did with Liam. Maybe it was the way he canvassed her up and down.

"So I imagine you enjoy amusement park rides, too. Ever been to Santa Monica Pier?" Liam wanted to know.

"No, I haven't."

"I think you and your daughter might enjoy it."

"Do you go often?" Sara asked, curious.

"Nope. Rock climbing is more my thing. But maybe you should try the pier sometime. Not in that outfit, though." He grinned. "Quite a difference from the way you looked Saturday night, but I like it. Wet chic."

She felt Jase tense beside her. He even took a step forward as if he was going to defend her honor...or something. But she clasped his arm. She didn't want trouble between Jase and Liam, so she changed the subject.

"What kind of food does the restaurant in Sacramento serve?"

"French gourmet. They even import truffles. And, of course, our wines are on their list."

"So this is business and pleasure?"

"Mostly pleasure. Friends are joining me."

"Well, enjoy your night on the town," she said, meaning it.

"I will. It was great to see you again, Sara. See you tomorrow, Jase." Then Liam was striding away toward the main house.

Jase muttered, "He has his eye on you."

"I think he has his eye on lots of women. I saw him charming them on Saturday night."

"Can he charm you?"

She was about to answer that no one seemed able to charm her but Jase, when Amy ran up to her and wrapped her arms around her legs. "I'm hungry, Mommy. When are we gonna eat?"

Sara glanced at Jase in his wet clothes, looking absolutely sexy with his T-shirt molded to his muscles, his jeans clinging to those powerful thighs. She was grateful for his help this afternoon, as well as the photographs he'd taken to remember the day. Well, she thought, in for a penny, in for a pound....

"I have a working grill out back," she said to him. "We were just going to grill some burgers."

"Pickles and tomatoes?" Amy asked, with a four-year-old's enthusiasm for a barbecue.

"With pickles and tomatoes and ketchup and mustard.

Care to join us?" she asked him lightly, as if it didn't matter if he said no.

"Payback for babysitting?" he asked.

She had to be honest. "Partly, but for some reason, I also enjoy talking to you."

"Talking?"

"Yes, talking. And that's what we're going to be doing over hamburgers."

He grinned at her. He actually grinned. "Give me five minutes to change clothes, and I'll do the grilling for you. You can put the rest of it together."

"Sounds good."

Being with Jase sounded good.

The swirl of ever-ticking thoughts ran through Jase's head as he stood at the grill behind the cottage, cooking burgers. His focus, however, wasn't on the burgers. It was on Amy...and Sara.

Sara was going to like the photos he'd shot of her and Amy. Maybe they'd make up for some of those she'd lost.

As Sara arranged plates and napkins on the table with Amy's help, Jase realized the sound of the little girl's laughter was a balm that soothed a deep ache he'd brought home with him from Africa. Even more so, Sara's understanding heart soothed that ache, too. What he didn't comprehend so well was the irritation and annoyance he'd felt when Liam had winked at Sara as if they'd established a relationship. Had they? Sara had had no problem making conversation with Liam. She hadn't actually been flirting—

Jase corralled his imagination. She had a right to associate with whomever she chose.

But he felt raw at the idea of her with Liam.

Memories of Dana had come rushing back in. All too well their breakup still played in his head.

He'd been in the hospital recovering. Another journalist he'd been friends with for years had stopped in to see him. They'd both known Dana. In fact, Peter had introduced them. After the preliminary small talk when Peter had assured him he'd make a complete recovery, Peter hadn't been his usual sarcastic self. Jase had felt the underlying tension and hadn't known what it meant.

Finally, Peter had said, "You know I've always been a straight shooter."

Jase had retorted, "Same here."

Peter had taken a photograph from his pocket, or rather a printout of a photograph. Before he'd handed it to Jase, he'd said, "Believe me, I don't want to show you this, but better me than someone else. If I could shoot this last week, then others have seen her, too. It will only be a matter of time until word gets around."

The journalistic community was a small world, even though they were scattered all over the continents. With emails, text messaging and social media, not much got by anybody.

Jase had been on painkillers, then. They hadn't been dulling the pain all that much or the absence of his fiancée whom he hadn't seen since a few weeks before he'd been shot. He'd had a premonition of what he was going to see in the photo and he'd braced himself as best he could.

The photograph was, of course, telling. With the Eiffel Tower in the background, Dana was kissing a man in a way that told anybody passing by this wasn't a brother or a friend. Peter had seen it and captured the shot.

"Two questions," Jase said.

"Go ahead."

"Does she know you saw her?"

"No. I didn't want her making up some kind of story,

and I wanted you to be prepared. What's the second question?"

"Who is he?"

"Do you really need to know that? Because I don't think it matters, really, who he is. She was shaken up by what happened to you."

"So shaken up she's kissing anybody these days?"

"Something like that. You know her, Jase. She's a risk taker. She likes danger. But she doesn't like anything bad to touch her."

"This didn't touch her, it touched *me*."

Peter just gave him a look.

"In other words, she's afraid I'll never be whole again?"

"I don't know what she's afraid of. Maybe you'd better ask her."

Dana had been on assignment. Though they had spoken once or twice on the phone, it had never occurred to him until then that if she really wanted a life with him, she would have been at his bedside.

Back then he hadn't known much about relationships. He hadn't known much about commitment. After all, he hadn't known his biological father, his mother had died of a drug overdose and he'd had three foster parents before Ethan had adopted him. What did he really know about relationships at all?

Except when Dana had walked into his hospital room a few days later, he'd known a relationship meant more than the opportunity to be unfaithful. He'd suddenly known that an engagement should mean building a life together, not living separate lives.

Dana had been flippant at first, avoiding his gaze, even jittery, which was unlike her. Under other circumstances, he might have suspected it was the hospital room and his condition. He was hooked up to IVs and monitors. His shoulder was wrapped and in a sling. Two ribs were broken, and he was still healing from a second abdominal surgery. That was enough to make any visitor jittery.

But he knew more than that was going on, and he wasn't going to play games. He told her to look in the drawer by the bedside table. When she did, she found the picture.

"Who took this?"

"Does it matter? Pictures don't lie, right? Pictures don't, but you've been."

"I don't know what to say, Jase."

It wasn't an "I'm sorry" or "It won't happen again" or "Can you forgive me?" Any of that might have revived feelings he'd once had. She simply said, "You have a long recovery process, here. I probably won't be back in the States for a few months."

"So my getting shot's the problem?"

"No, but when you got shot, I started thinking. You talk about kids as if you want to have them someday. You relate to them like I can't. I don't want to be a mother. I want to stay in the life I have. But the way you talk about your father's vineyard sometimes, I think you want more than a life as a photojournalist."

"I know I want to be involved with someone who knows how to be faithful."

"You deserve someone who knows how to be faithful. Obviously that person isn't me. I turned to someone else because I was upset about you…about everything I'd realized about *us*…how we're different in things that matter."

Although he'd felt bitterness and resentment and betrayal, they hadn't parted as enemies. What was the point? If nothing else, Jase was a practical man. Still…*that* photograph was etched in his mind.

He thought about everything Dana had said as he watched Sara showing Amy precisely where to put the napkin. Exactly what *did* he want from Sara? What did she want from him?

As she and Amy sat at the table to wait for the burgers, she dished out broccoli salad she already had prepared, and baked beans that she'd doctored with bacon and brown sugar, onion and celery. She'd told him she liked to cook and putter in the kitchen. He liked the idea of a woman who enjoyed doing that.

"Almost ready," he said over his shoulder.

"I read the new brochure you laid on the table. It really captures everything about the vineyard. Did you write the copy, too?"

"I did," he said, flipping the burgers onto a plate and bringing them to the table. "Photos of something unique to Raintree weren't in the brochure—hot springs. We don't tell the general public about them."

"But you're telling me."

"If you're up to a four-wheeler ride and a hike, we could go see them. Anytime you want to go, just say the word."

He knew the hot springs setting. He knew it could be a place for romance. But whether Sara wanted that or not was still in question.

When he settled across the table from her, his knee brushed hers. She didn't move away, and she did meet his direct eye contact when she said, "I will."

Jase knew if they ever went to those hot springs, they'd return to Raintree as much more than friends.

## Chapter Eight

Around one, Sara took her lunch out back at the PT center and sat at one of the picnic tables. Doing so brought back memories of last night and having burgers on the grill with Jase…Jase playing hopscotch with Amy…Jase in a wet T-shirt.

To distract herself from going there, she pulled out her cell phone. There was a text message from Marissa. She simply said, Call me.

So Sara did. When Marissa answered, she asked, "Did you see it or hear about it?"

"About what?"

"Today, the article about The Mommy Club was in the paper. It's on the newspaper's website, too, and there are comments already."

Sara didn't have mobile web access on her phone. "Good comments?"

"Mostly good. They're about other drop-off points for

food and clothes, contributors wanting a list of items The Mommy Club really needs and requesting more info about Thrifty Solutions. But most of all, there are comments from readers who want women's stories."

"Uh-oh."

"Yeah, that's what I thought."

"Jase asked me if I'd let him interview me."

"Me, too, but I said no. I just can't, not with wanting to keep Jordan's father from knowing about him."

"That would be a terrible way for him to find out."

"It's not going to happen," Marissa said with vehement determination.

"My fire story is already public. Not the insurance investigation. I'm sure the insurance company doesn't want *that* public, any more than I do. So if Jase just wrote about the fire and moving into the cottage, and all the help The Mommy Club gave me, we could keep the focus on that. If he can find others who were helped and will talk about it, the point of the article wouldn't be just on me but the organization."

When Marissa didn't respond right away, Sara admitted, "I know there's a chance everything can come out, but I haven't done anything wrong. Maybe my story can help someone else."

"You're braver than I am."

"Not brave. Maybe I just have less to lose."

Those same words echoed in Sara's head that night when Jase came over to the cottage. She suspected he might. After she'd put Amy to bed, she'd stayed dressed herself. To give her courage? Backbone? Resistance where he was concerned?

She was beginning to realize that Jase Cramer was a temptation like no other she'd ever had. She'd never skipped from relationship to relationship. In fact, Conrad had been her first real serious involvement. With Conrad, passion hadn't been a driving force. She'd wanted to love and have him love her back. Conrad had been older and more experienced. Since she'd lost her parents, she'd felt adrift and Conrad had anchored her. But had her values and Conrad's ever meshed? Maybe she'd married him for all the wrong reasons.

Insight that had come too late. She'd never be sorry she'd married Conrad. She'd had Amy. But she did have regrets that she and Conrad had never had the intimate kind of relationship they should have both craved.

Now she was beginning to crave it. She was beginning to crave Jase.

He didn't talk about the article at first, rather he handed her a manila envelope. "See what you think," he said with a crooked smile that urged her to forget all about good sense and dive into his arms.

"Cookies and milk?" she asked. "Or…I just happen to have a very good bottle of wine."

He laughed. "The cookies and milk sound great. By the way, my dad enjoyed the ones you baked. I told him he should thank you himself, but—" Jase shrugged. "Parents aren't any easier to control than kids."

She supposed that was the truth all children came to face, as well as parents.

After they were seated on the sofa, she opened the envelope and pulled out the contents. There were six pieces of photographic paper with two prints on each. Underneath those, she found the article that had appeared in the paper. That, she set aside for the time being. She couldn't wait to see the prints.

Immediately she was entranced by them. Amy's expressions were priceless as she played hopscotch, ran in the spray of the hose and grinned up at Sara as if she were the best mother in the world. "Oh, Jase, these are beautiful."

"They did come out well, didn't they?" he said with some self-satisfaction. "I guess I haven't altogether lost my touch."

"You haven't lost your touch one little bit, and you know it. You take wonderful photographs of scenery, but people and especially children are your specialty."

"I have more of you and Amy. I'm going to send the whole batch to the printing house I use. Then you can start a new photo album. You'll have to get a point-and-shoot camera so you can add to it."

She studied the photographs again. They all meant so much to her. "You are a kind man."

"Maybe, or maybe I have an ulterior motive."

"Such as?"

"Not what you're thinking." His smile was rakish. "If we ever do go to bed together, it will be because we both want it. I guess I just want to give you back something you lost, the way you gave me back something I lost. You've got a great smile, Sara. I see it with Amy all the time. But other times, I just sense sadness."

"You're wrong."

"No, I don't think I am. You not only regret what happened in your marriage, I think you regret your marriage."

"I loved Conrad. We had Amy. How could I regret that?"

"Maybe that was a bad choice of words. But don't you wonder what might have happened if you'd married someone else?"

She looked away and shrugged. "The grass is always greener."

"Sara, it's not a sin to wonder what you could have done differently."

She looked back to him. "No, it's not, but I can't change my history. So the best thing to do is learn from it and move on."

"*Are* you moving on?"

They stared at each other for at least ten very long seconds. She felt battered by his conclusions and questions as if she'd been tossed in a storm of wrong decisions…wrong moves…wrong choices.

And if she'd been wrong before, she could be wrong again.

"Did you come over tonight to ask probing personal questions or to give me the pictures?"

"I came over because I wanted to see you…because I wanted to do this."

He moved so fast and took advantage of her surprise so masterfully that she didn't even know she was responding until she heard herself moan, until his possessiveness claimed her, until his kiss became deep and hungry and totally consuming.

Jase was more than temptation. He was passion, excitement and everything she'd ever longed for and hadn't known. That's why he was so hard to resist. That's why she was kissing him back, responding as if her life depended on it.

When Jase ended the kiss, she tried to clear her head but he nuzzled her neck and she was still caught up in his touch.

"The earth shakes when you kiss me," she finally managed to murmur.

"And fireworks explode?" he asked with a throaty, sexy chuckle.

She didn't answer and he stopped nuzzling her neck. Hooking his thumb under her chin, he turned her face toward his. "What are you thinking?"

"I'm wondering where we go from here."

"Do you always need a plan?"

"I have a daughter."

"I'm not forgetting that."

Jase ran his hand over his face as if he needed a moment. Then he said, "I did come over for another reason. Have you considered letting me interview you?"

"I've been thinking about it all evening. I saw the comments on the newspaper's website."

"Marissa still won't budge. Kaitlyn is on the fence. I do have another mother of two, Ann Custer, whose husband is in Afghanistan. I'm doing her interview tomorrow."

Sara thought about it a last time. "We can stick to the fire and moving into the cottage here?"

"Yes, but I'd also like to mention you're a widow and single mom. That's The Mommy Club lead-in. I'd like your thoughts and feelings on losing things you held dear. I'd like you to express how you felt when you saw volunteers carrying in everything you might need."

"You want me to turn myself inside out."

"A part of yourself, maybe. Not everything."

No, not everything. Not for the article. But maybe for him. He was looking at her as if he expected no less than her best. He was looking at her as if he wanted to make love to her right here…right now.

"Jase…"

"Why don't you just start talking? Remember as best you can the fear when you smelled the smoke and tell me what came next." He took out his phone, pressed an app she assumed was a recorder and nodded.

She started with the smoke.

An hour later, she felt more exhausted than she could ever express. Remembering waking up unable to catch her breath, immediately stricken because Amy seemed so far away, had brought back fear and panic that had almost made her break out in a sweat. Only Jase's voice and the next question had kept her in the here and now. Until he probed again and she'd relived the house burning down in front of her eyes. It had gotten easier after that, but still...

After Jase attached his phone to the holster on his belt, he moved closer to her and wrapped his arm around her.

She would have pulled away if they kissed again. Tonight she wasn't sure she could resist making love with him.

Making love with all its consequences.

"Settle down," he urged her, holding her a little tighter. "I know what it's like to tell your story. Remember, *I* did it with *you*."

Tucking her head against Jase's shoulder, she didn't think anything had ever felt so right.

That thought scared her as much as telling her story to the world.

Sara arrived to work early the next morning, still remembering the strong feel of Jase's arms around her, the way he represented comfort as well as temptation. He hadn't kissed her again, though he'd looked as if he wanted to. And she *had* wanted him to. But at some point, neither of them would stop, and they had to be prepared for the repercussions of that.

Since she was a few minutes early, curiosity drove her to the newspaper's website and Jase's article. There were more comments now. She ran her gaze over the list and then froze at a whole batch of them. It took her a moment to realize the thread was discussing *her*.

*Interested Party in Fawn Grove* mentioned the story on the news about her house burning down. The person went on to state The Mommy Club brigade had gathered furniture for her.

That was fine, but someone else said, Where did all the furniture go?

A new comment by *Gossip Lady* stated, I heard Sara Stevens is staying at Raintree Winery.

*Bystander* listed a link to the winery's social media page and said, See discussion there. Really interesting.

Sara knew she should walk away from the computer. She knew she shouldn't care what was being said. But this could affect Amy as well as her. It could affect Jase and business at the winery. Had he realized that might happen? Or had it been part of his plan to get publicity for Raintree?

No, that wasn't Jase.

But she remembered when Conrad's car had been repossessed and the thoughts that had rolled through her head then. *This must be a mistake. Conrad would have told me if we were in trouble.*

So, yes, she had doubts about her judgment in men. She clicked on the link.

She was appalled at the discussion on the winery's social media page. Someone named *Orange Maiden* posed the question, Just where at the winery is Sara Stevens staying?

*SunnyGirl*'s response to that was, Maybe at the main house. Maybe she has more on her mind than a temporary place to live. After all, Jase Cramer is a very eligible bachelor.

That comment alone could fuel Ethan Cramer's belief that she was a gold digger!

Now Sara did stop reading and picked up the phone, speed dialing Jase's number.

He answered immediately. "You saw the comments," he said matter-of-factly.

"Yes, I saw the comments, and I don't like them. What are we going to do about this?"

"I don't see that there's anything we *can* do except to go ahead with the interview."

"You're kidding, right?"

"I'm serious, Sara. The questions raised will be laid to rest by my interviewing you."

"Jase, I just…I don't know what to do. I don't want people to get the wrong impression about me."

"They won't. Let me write up the interview and let the newspaper run it."

"I need some time to think about it. Can you give me that?"

"I'll hold the article for now. But I don't think that's the best thing to do."

They were going to have to agree to disagree on this one because she wasn't ready to go public with her life.

The following Monday, Sara picked up Amy and Jordan at day care. After carrying Jordan inside the winery offices to Marissa, she set him on his feet.

Spotting them, Marissa clapped her hands. "Come here, honey."

Jordan had taken his first steps over the weekend, and he now babbled and smiled and walked toward his mommy with an exuberant, if halting, gait.

"At the day care they said he was walking everywhere he could today," Sara explained.

Marissa clasped her son in her arms.

Amy looked up at Sara. "Can I draw?"

"Stay a few minutes," Marissa suggested to Sara. "We haven't talked since Jase's article drew so many comments."

The front door opened and Liam came in. After a

"hello" to them both, he handed Marissa flyers. "These show what our competitors are doing."

Marissa thanked him.

Amy pulled on Sara's arm. "*Can* I draw, Mommy?"

After a look at Marissa, Sara suggested to her daughter, "I think you can draw at home."

Home. She reminded herself she couldn't think of the cottage that way.

"Did I interrupt something?" Liam asked, perceptive enough to sense the unfinished conversation between her and Marissa.

"We were about to have a discussion about the comments concerning Sara online," Marissa responded honestly.

Sara shook her head, indicating she didn't want to talk about it.

But Liam easily picked up the idea and the thread. "Jase told me he interviewed you. When's that coming out?"

"I don't know if I want him to go ahead with it."

"You want rumors floating out there about you living here and your motives?" Liam asked with a penetrating look that surprised her. He wasn't all charm, now, but blunt honesty.

"Of course not. But I also don't want to feed more rumors."

"Without putting rumors to rest in Jase's interview, there's supposition, Sara," Marissa said softly. "With your job, do you really want that?"

Could her job be in jeopardy if the rumor mill really got going?

With a wave toward the door, Liam gestured to the outside world. "People are going to say what they want, no matter what the truth is. They talk and make up things and spread rumors. That's just the way of life in a small town like Fawn Grove. Don't you think I know people talk about me in unflattering ways? I'm not the lady-killer everybody thinks I am," he admitted with some chagrin.

Sara had to smile. "You're not?"

Scowling at her, he said decisively, "No. Sure, I don't stick around much with any one woman. I'm just not the sticking-around type. But if I were the Casanova everybody says I am, I'd be too exhausted to make wine. The thing is—there's a difference between me and you. *I* don't care what everybody thinks. But *you* do. Right?"

Yes, she cared, because she had clients who had to believe in her, because she wanted Amy to be proud of her, because she didn't want anything negative to touch her daughter.

"This is the way I see it," Liam went on. "All you can do is put the truth out there. It won't hurt to provide the public with it and you might be doing other women a service. Jase is a wonderful journalist. If anyone can sell your story, he can. Maybe you should let him give it a try."

When Sara glanced at Marissa, Marissa nodded. "I agree with Liam. Jase knows how to slant an interview. You know that. Give him a chance with yours."

Should she give Jase Cramer that chance?

Holding Amy's hand, Sara strolled with her daughter through Raintree's Wine and Music Festival on Saturday afternoon. The event was a landscape of color, sounds and scents. Chefs in canopied booths offered delicacies from lobster tails to egg rolls to endive wraps stuffed with goat cheese. Miniature orange trees as well as trellises laced with flowers separated the booths and led the guests along pathways, where they could sample food and wine in a garden-party atmosphere.

Her daughter seemed to be enjoying their stroll, too, as

she pointed and chattered and played with a yellow balloon tied to one of the booths. Sara was looking for Marissa, who'd planned much of the festival, when she felt a hand on her shoulder. Turning, she found Rodney Herkfeld, who had been a friend of Conrad's.

"I thought that was you," he said with a huge smile. "I haven't seen you since…"

*Conrad's funeral,* Sara finished in her mind.

He remembered, too, but didn't say the words. Instead he said, "It doesn't matter when I last saw you. It's been too long. I read that article in the paper and the follow-up conversation online. That's one of the reasons I came today. I wanted to see how you were."

Her worst fears had materialized. More people than she'd expected had read the comments online. "I guess everyone knows I'm living here. In the cottage behind the main house," she added for good measure, wanting him to know the truth.

"It's hard to keep anything quiet in Fawn Grove. You do know that, don't you? Conrad told me you moved here for a position before you were married, so you haven't lived here all your life. But small towns are small towns."

How often had she heard *that* in the past week? Maybe because it was true.

He looked uncomfortable for a moment, then said, "I'm sorry about everything that happened to Conrad. As the store's accountant, I was aware of his financial problems, but there was nothing I could do to help him turn things around. The store he managed was headed downhill because of the bigger chains. He did the best he could and I wanted you to know that."

Conrad might have done the best he could with the store, but Rodney didn't know about the lies. Rodney didn't know how betrayed she'd felt because her husband hadn't shared his problems with her.

Suddenly Kaitlyn appeared, strolling down the path, looking like a model. Casual and classy, she was dressed in a summer-flowered sheath with white sandals. Her gold earrings glinted in the sun. When she caught Sara's eye, it was as if she was asking a question. Sara answered it by waving to her.

Taking the cue, Kaitlyn approached Sara and Rodney.

After introductions, Rodney said, "I just want to give you my card." He slipped it to Sara. "If you need any help with numbers or budgets or taxes, give me a call. I mean it, Sara. I couldn't help Conrad, but I'd like to help you."

A jazz band began playing and Rodney gestured to it. "Ah, the music's started. What a wonderful place these festivals can be. I hear they're starting with jazz, leading into the forties, then going up the decades with the music we all loved most. That could have some guests staying here all day. I'm going to sample more of the food. Sara, it was good to see you. Dr. Foster, nice to meet you."

After Rodney had ambled away, Kaitlyn glanced around. "Everyone's not only eating, but sampling the wine. These festivals help sales, no doubt about it. The guests not only buy for themselves, but for their friends and families, too. They'll buy wines for birthdays and Christmases." She took a sip from the wineglass she held and savored the taste. "There are companies trying to bottle wines the same way companies make soda. It's just not possible. As long as Raintree keeps their wines pure to the idea they had when they began, they will never make run-of-the-mill wines."

"You sound as if you know a lot about it," Sara said.

"My husband was in marketing for a rival winery."

That was the first Sara had heard anything mentioned about Kaitlyn's past life.

"Let's go over here and get you a balloon," Kaitlyn said to Amy. "I know one of the chefs. I'm sure he wouldn't mind a balloon missing from his display."

Sara led Amy over to a booth where Kaitlyn exchanged a few words with the chef making a delicious-looking fried crab ball. She plucked a light blue balloon from the array flying toward the sky. Opening her purse, she found a ribbon there. She tied the balloon onto it, made a little loop so it would be easier for Amy to hold on to or slip her hand into. Then she gave the balloon to her.

"Here you go."

"You're so good with kids," Sara complimented her.

This time, when she gazed at Kaitlyn's eyes, she saw sadness there, something she hadn't noticed before. As they strolled through a throng of people and found an empty bench, they sat and Amy bobbed her balloon up and down.

Sara asked, "Are you going to let Jase interview you for an article?"

Kaitlyn, usually a decisive person, looked undecided. "I'm weighing the possibility, but I don't like the idea."

"I know what you mean. But I think I've come to the conclusion that I'd like the truth out there, and maybe my story will help someone else."

"We all have stories, and none are easy to tell."

"Do you tell yours often?"

"Hardly ever. Even Jase doesn't know why I'm so involved in The Mommy Club."

"Do you want to tell me?" Sara asked gently, wondering if Kaitlyn needed a friend just like everyone else.

She hesitated, then said in a low tone, "My husband and I had a premature baby who didn't make it. Preeclampsia snuck up on me. Because I was a doctor, my husband thought I should have realized what was happening sooner. Maybe I should have."

Sara clasped Kaitlyn's hand. "I'm so sorry. I just can't imagine losing a baby."

"Neither could I. I was in a deep funk afterward, and Tom and I grew further and further apart. He asked for a divorce. I suggested counseling, but he didn't want any part of that. Looking back, I have so many regrets."

"Just as all of us have a story, I guess we all have regrets, too."

"I don't know what I would have done without The Mommy Club. I went to a support group and someone there mentioned it. I started out by helping new moms. I figured if I helped others, I'd get better, and that pretty much happened. I had a purpose in my practice, but The Mommy Club gave me a purpose *outside* of my practice. I needed that."

"So if you do an interview with Jase, you're wondering how much to say."

"Exactly," Kaitlyn agreed.

Amy suddenly jumped off the bench and ran to the tall, broad-shouldered man in the red polo shirt and chinos who was walking toward them with a camera hanging around his neck.

Jase smiled broadly, scooped her up in his arms and spun her in a circle as her balloon bobbed above them both.

"He's daddy material," Kaitlyn suggested with a sly smile.

Was Jase really daddy material? Was she ready to accept another man into her life when her marriage had seemed to go so wrong?

Jase's gaze found hers over Amy's head. The wine festival faded away. Maybe it *was* time to explore more than an interview with Jase Cramer.

## Chapter Nine

Jase approached Sara with Amy, then set the little girl on the ground. Before Amy could blink, he waved his hand in back of her daughter's ear and pulled out a shiny pink barrette.

"Look, Mommy! For my hair."

"I see. Do you want me to put it in?"

Her daughter stood still as Sara attached the barrette in the soft strands over Amy's temple. Kaitlyn offered her hand to Amy. "Why don't we go to the face-painting booth and see what you'd like?"

Amy looked up at Sara. "Can I?"

"Sure, I'll be right with you."

Amy happily trotted off with Kaitlyn, not even throwing a glance over her shoulder.

"She's easy to please," Jase said with a smile.

"You do a good job of it. Pink barrettes and little girls just go together."

An awkward silence ensued and Sara knew she was the one who had to break it. "The festival is great."

"Marissa could be an event planner anywhere. I'd better think about giving her a raise or I might lose her."

"She feels she owes a lot to you. I don't think you'll lose her."

"I didn't do anything but give her a job and a chance. She's made the most of it."

An uncomfortable silence again settled between them and Sara told Jase what she'd decided about living at the cottage. "I haven't heard anything from the insurance investigator yet so I want to start paying you rent."

He gave her a look that said he was about to refuse, but then he kept silent. Finally he said, "If that's what you feel you have to do."

"That's not the only thing I feel I have to do. I've been thinking about the interview you did with me. If you still want to write it up, go ahead. I'm okay with it."

His gray gaze was probing. "What changed your mind?"

"Lots of things. But most of all I realized I don't want someone else defining me. I want to put out the truth. If that's not enough, so be it. I have to at least try. And getting word out about The Mommy Club is important. Your article was the first some people even heard about it."

"It's Fawn Grove's best kept secret. People who give help don't like to toot their own horn. People who accept help don't like to admit it."

"That makes sense."

Sara knew she didn't want to step away from Jase. She wanted to spend more time with him, to see if he liked being with her and Amy. "I suppose you have to mingle." She didn't know what Jase's duties might be today.

"I do, but not all the time. What do you have in mind?"

"I thought we might enjoy the music together, let Amy run around and get really tired, eat ourselves silly."

"I can't think of a better way to spend the afternoon." The look in his eyes said he meant it.

As Sara walked side by side with Jase that afternoon, visiting each stand, listening to music, tasting food they all liked to eat, sitting on a bench under a canvas canopy, sampling gourmet ice cream, she and Jase talked about everything. He didn't seem to mind being interrupted by Amy. He didn't seem to mind a drip of ice cream on his arm or making time for a four-year-old. Throughout it, he somehow found a way to make Sara feel special, the focus of his attention.

"There's one more thing I want you to try," he said with a twinkle in his eyes.

"I'm stuffed," Sara protested, as Amy curled up beside her, the sun and activity taking its toll.

"Be right back."

When Jase returned, he held a dish of pastries that had been dipped in chocolate.

Sara groaned. "I won't fit in my scrubs."

He looked her up and down. "You'll fit in your scrubs just fine. The outside isn't the best part. The inside has a mixture of mascarpone cheese and peanut butter cream. Carlo's known for these. Diners go to his restaurant just for the dessert. Come on, open up."

Jase was seated on the other side of her now, looking at her with mischief in his eyes. This was a side of him she didn't see enough of. She opened her mouth and he offered her a bite of the pastry, his gaze never leaving hers. She felt breathless, transported to intimacy only the two of them could share. How was that possible by just looking at him?

When she took a bite of the pastry, his thumb grazed her lip. She felt a tremor ripple through her, and he must have felt it, too, because his eyes darkened. As he fed her the rest of the pastry, some of the filling escaped onto his thumb. He offered it to her. She took a quick lick, and he pulled his hand away.

"What do you think?" he asked in a husky voice.

"I think this pastry is absolutely decadent."

"Want another?" he teased.

"I think you should try one." She picked one up and fed it to him.

When he'd finished, he clasped her hand and said in a low voice, "Feeding each other could get us into a lot of trouble."

"I don't think we need to feed each other to get into trouble."

"You know what I'd like to do right now, don't you?"

"Maybe."

She glanced down at her dozing daughter, laid her hand on her head, then brushed her hair to one side.

Turning her focus back to Jase, she said, "I've been thinking about those hot springs."

"You have?" he asked blandly, waiting for her to go on.

"I'd like to visit them with you."

After a few heartbeats, he asked, "Do you have a bathing suit?"

"I picked one up at Thrifty Solutions after our evening with the hose."

"How about tomorrow?" he suggested.

"I'll have to check with Marissa to see if she can watch Amy. I'll let you know as soon as I find her."

"Why don't we go find her together? I can carry Amy back to the cottage for you, but then I do have to come back here to the festival."

"I understand."

Jase had that look in his eyes again, a look that told her their visit to the hot springs could indeed get very hot.

Sara hadn't known that Raintree kept four-wheelers on the property, but it made sense. Such a vehicle made it easier to get around anyplace on the vineyard. Marissa had come over with Jordan, insisting he could sleep anywhere, and gave her a thumbs-up when Jase pulled up outside.

Sara had worn a swimsuit under her jeans and T-shirt. After all, she didn't know how far they'd have to hike to reach the hot springs.

There was a cooler strapped to the back of the four-wheeler, and Sara motioned to it before she climbed in. "A picnic?"

"Cold water to drink is always good when you dunk in hot springs. I also packed baguette slices, fruit and cheese."

She climbed in beside him. "How far will we have to hike?"

"I can get us pretty close. We'll have to return home before nightfall, though. I know my way back, but I don't want to take that chance driving it if you're with me."

She found that statement both comforting and scary. "So you'd take a risk if I weren't with you?"

"I think we're talking about more than a trip in the four-wheeler." He sounded a bit wary.

"I just know you risked your life before you were injured. I wondered if you'd put yourself in the same danger again."

"Uh-oh. Why do I have the feeling this dip into a geo-thermal pool isn't going to be all pleasurable?"

"Isn't the purpose of tonight to get to know each other better?"

"Don't you know me well enough?"

She didn't know if she did. How long might it take for

her to forget about everything that happened with Conrad? How long might it take for her to be willing to take a risk with Jase?

They rode through the vineyards with late-June evening scents warmed by the sun drifting by them—wild grasses and sage. After a while, the landscape changed from rolling hills to rockier terrain. This area of the property seemed untouched, pristine in its earthiness. They circled red-brown rocks honed by the weather that had probably been there for centuries.

The sounds from the four-wheeler made conversation spotty, but when Jase slowed, he said, "I used to come exploring out here. At one point, I thought I might want to be a geologist…along with a magician."

He'd obviously had many dreams as a kid. Which ones did he want to come true now? "But you ended up photographing all this instead, right?"

"I did. It made me curious about tectonic plates, thermal springs, mineral waters. We could probably turn this into a resort if we wanted to, but my dad wanted to keep this area natural. The year before I went to college, we did some work on it. Or rather, he supervised and I worked with some other guys. We dug out the trail that leads to the hot springs pool and sculptured the surrounding area. When we built up the walls around the hot spring, we fashioned steps leading down into it. It's not quite as primitive as it once was."

"Does anyone ever come out here?"

"Rarely. We have a service maintain it. Actually, when I was finished with my rehab, I drove out here a lot. Soaking in the waters seemed to help. Maybe that's just a mind game I played, but my muscles would loosen up. Afterward I could stretch them and exercise them better."

"I wish you had told me about this while you were in PT."

"Why?"

"Because I definitely would have encouraged you."

"Well, you can encourage me now."

The look he gave her sent a thrill through her, a thrill that she told herself she was ready for. She did need to live her life and forget about everything that had happened with Conrad. With Amy being looked after, tonight she was free to be a woman, to be herself, to really taste life again and enjoy it.

They followed a gravel path that had been groomed for the vehicle. Jase pulled up beside an outcropping of rocks that hid the area beyond. She could spot the footpath that circled around the rocks, and her heart began beating really fast.

After Jase pulled the cooler from the back of the vehicle, he joined her at the path. Handing her a blanket and towels, he said, "We might need these, and you might need a hand over the rocks, so we're better balanced this way."

She wondered what kind of bathing suit he was wearing under his jeans, and how he'd look when he slipped them off. She was thinking about touching his skin, smelling his scent, being close to him. A blanket, towels, swimsuits and water all equaled intimacy.

After he studied her for a few moments, he said blandly, "This could just be a dip in the hot springs, you know. Relax, Sara. When you have a thought, it flashes like a neon sign in your eyes. I don't suppose you play poker well."

"Is that a compliment or an insult?" She couldn't tell from Jase's tone.

"Definitely a compliment. Remember, I was engaged to a woman who was able to hide too much."

Yes, she did remember. More than anything she remembered the pain in his voice when he'd told her about it, the monumental betrayal he'd felt, the sense that he'd hoped for a dream he could never have.

"You like women who take risks, don't you?" she asked quietly. He'd been an adventurer at heart and she suspected he'd like that quality in the women he became involved with.

"I did…once. But now I'm older and wiser," he joked.

"Wiser, maybe, but not that old."

Jase just smiled one of those enigmatic smiles, then offered her his hand as they started up the path. His grip on hers was firm and masterful. He knew where he was going and probably what he wanted to do. She wouldn't be a tease, that's for sure. If they started something, she would finish it.

The path became narrower. Instead of leading her, however, Jase dropped in back of her. "Just follow the yellow markers," he said. "If I climb behind you, I can catch you if you fall."

Actually, that was a wonderful idea—a man who would catch her if she fell. For the longest time she'd felt alone. Even when she and Conrad were married, she'd felt she had full responsibility for Amy, for her emotional and physical welfare. Since Conrad's death, the financial burden had been even heavier and she'd worried day and night about giving Amy the life she needed, the life she deserved. She was an independent woman and she wanted to stay independent, no doubt about that. But it would be so nice to feel that she wasn't alone.

With the blanket and towels under her arm, Sara made her way without too much difficulty. Suddenly, however, as she was climbing a rock a little higher than the rest, her sneaker slipped. She felt her legs go out from under her. She heard a thunk and then she was suspended in strong, muscular arms that seemed to know how to keep a woman safe.

She gazed up at Jase and was mesmerized by what she saw in his eyes. It was desire and hunger and an intense passion for life that she'd been drawn to in him from the very beginning.

But she didn't want him to know how much. She couldn't let her guard down completely and still protect herself and Amy.

Trying to capture her composure once more, she teased, "I suppose that was the cooler that fell?"

"Everything's safe in there. I know how to pack."

The question on the tip of her tongue was, *Am I safe with you?* But she couldn't ask it. Even if she asked it, she didn't know if she'd believe his answer.

"I'm always thanking you," she murmured.

"And I always tell you, no thanks are necessary. Here, let's just put you on top of that rock so you don't have to scramble over it."

After he'd set her on a level spot, she anchored the towels and blanket under her arm once more and realized her legs were shaky as she took her next step. Being in Jase's arms always made her feel that way. But she kept going because she didn't want him to notice.

Sara was surprised when she reached a summit and saw the footpath was going to take her down again.

"It's not much farther," Jase told her. "Look down and to your right and you can see the reflection on the water."

The sun's late-day rays caught and danced on a pool about ten feet below.

"Oh, Jase, this is like some untouched world."

"Not so untouched. We've put a few solar lights around, smoothed rock where it needed to be smoothed, made the pool safe. I've photographed it often at different times of the day, but I don't make any of those photographs public. We don't want anyone asking, 'Where is it and how can I get there?'"

"I can understand that."

They descended the elongated, wide rock steps until they stood at the rim of the pool. "How deep is it?" she asked, mesmerized by the bubbling water.

"About four feet. We have a rock ledge along one side to sit on."

"I have a suit on under my jeans." She didn't turn to meet his eyes.

But his voice came from over her right shoulder. "So do I." He took her by the shoulders and turned her around. "You are going to make eye contact, right?"

The twinkle in his eyes made her smile. "I suppose that's the best way to have a conversation."

He laughed. "So how do you want to do this? Fruit and cheese now or later?"

"Later."

"Okay. I'll just grab the bottles of water and lay out the blanket. When we get out, we'll have someplace to dry off."

Jase's back was to her when Sara lifted off her T-shirt. She was wearing a two-piece suit. Some would call it a bikini but it was definitely more than strings. When she'd found it at Thrifty Solutions, it still had tags on it and she wondered who had donated it. She just knew that someday she wanted to be the one who could donate to Thrifty Solutions, who could help other moms through The Mommy Club. The neon turquoise color of the suit shimmered in the sun and she wondered what Jase would think of her in it.

He'd turned around by the time she was unfastening

her jeans. He made no attempt to avert his eyes, because he obviously enjoyed the sight.

"You're making me self-conscious," she said.

"I won't tell you what you're making me."

Heat rushed to her cheeks and she knew that was silly. She wasn't a teenager in high school, and she'd worn plenty of bathing suits in her lifetime. But tonight… Tonight just seemed different.

Jase quickly discarded his boots, jeans and shirt, and now *she* was the one doing the looking…and thinking ahead to a kiss that didn't end. Jase was wearing board-shorts, plain green that rode low on his hips. The drawstring was tied just below his navel. The scars across his shoulder and along his abdomen were noticeable but they didn't snag her attention long as her gaze drifted to his powerful thighs, the dark hair on his legs, his very masculine stance.

Offering her his hand to help her down into the pool, he said, "Be careful. The rocks can be slippery."

They were, but she was careful and soon she was sitting on the ledge. From a rocky shelf, Jase picked up two bottles of water, uncapped them and offered her one. Maybe he was just trying to put her more at ease, but she took one, drank a few long swallows, then set it back on the shelf.

The water surrounding them was deliciously warm. It swirled around them as if propelled by jets.

"Why did you decide to come up here with me today?" Jase suddenly asked.

She hadn't expected that question. But as he'd noticed, she had trouble hiding her feelings. She told him honestly, "I ran into someone at the festival from my old life."

"By 'old life,' you mean before your husband died?"

"Yes. It was his store's accountant."

After a brief pause, Jase guessed, "And he told you he tried to warn your husband about his financial trouble."

Jase had been around long enough to realize how life worked. "Yes. He told me Conrad tried to do his best with the store, but he just couldn't make the business grow."

"You said your husband was older than you."

"About fifteen years older."

"Why were you attracted to someone older?"

"Jase, I didn't come here tonight to talk about Conrad."

"No, but you said you wanted to get to know me and I want to get to know you. Were you madly attracted to him?"

Her breath caught as she thought about the feelings she'd once had for Conrad, and how they compared to her growing feelings for Jase. "No, it wasn't like that. I mean, yes, I was attracted to him, but in a quiet way. I'd lost my parents and I had no family. Conrad had no family, either. We met near the holidays and we started talking about feeling lonely. Suddenly we were spending Christmas together."

"So he represented safety and stability you didn't have."

Hadn't she come to that conclusion herself? "I guess you could say that. Do you mind if I ask you about your fiancée?"

"Tit for tat?"

"No, just curious. Do you still think about her? Do you wonder what would have happened if you hadn't been injured?"

"I'd say that was true up until about a year ago."

"What happened then?"

"One of our wines won an award. I realized I'd been instrumental in helping make that happen. Not only as far as the mix of grapes, but a new, more organic process, and marketing it to the right restaurants. That night I started looking ahead rather than back."

"That's what I want to do."

As Jase studied her, she felt he was trying to read her deeper than anybody had ever read her before. He must have seen what he was looking for because he moved closer, dropped his arm around her shoulders and bent his head to kiss her.

The first press of his lips on hers was light and tentative. He was waiting for her signal of acceptance.

Warm water lapped at her midriff as she leaned into him, needing to feel his skin against hers. That was all the encouragement he obviously needed, because as she parted her lips, he thrust inside, kissing her in a way he hadn't before. Somehow it was more sensual, more seductive, more *everything*. Heat and water and a private world curled around them, insulating and protecting them against outside forces. There were no responsibilities, no consequences, no regrets. Just her and Jase in an untouched world.

When he broke the kiss, he didn't move away. She'd clipped her hair on top of her head and he nuzzled her neck, tongued her earlobe, making her altogether restless and wanting. As his hands slid to the back of her top, she knew exactly what he was doing. She knew exactly what *she* was doing.

He unhooked it to let it flow to the side of the pool. Then he lifted her chin to his, gazed into her eyes and touched her breast. It was so erotic looking at him that way while he trailed his fingers around and around, pressed his palm into her and then fingered her nipple. She moaned and he laughed, and any vestige of restraint dropped away.

As he kissed her again, still giving attention to her breast, she wondered how she could feel this much passion and this much need. Where had these feelings been all her life? Why hadn't sensual need ever been a priority before? When she was with Jase, all she thought about was being close to him, touching him, kissing him.

He slid his hand under her and scooped her up onto his lap. He was obviously aroused and she felt lost in the moment rather than in what came next. One hand held her to him while the other edged the fabric of her bikini bottom and tugged it down.

"Jase."

"You're safe," he murmured. "Relax and trust me."

This moment was everything. His fingers trailed down her backside, making a path up her thigh, putting her in an erotic trance. He still kissed her and touched her and brought pleasure everywhere. She found herself paralyzed to do anything but enjoy his next caress, his next kiss, his next touch. His thumb became an instrument of pleasure as he circled, teased, titillated.

She ran her hands over his chest and curled her fingers into his shoulders. He was escalating the tension in her body, making all of her muscles wind tight, expecting some kind of release. The headiness of what they were doing almost made her dizzy. Her breath came faster, and finally he touched her where she wanted to be touched most. He wasn't filling her, but he was—

The orgasm hit her, surprising her, exciting her, carrying her to the edges of sublime, until all she could do was hold on to Jase, hoping she didn't come apart in his arms. She tried to catch her breath and as she gazed into his eyes, she felt more vulnerable than she'd ever felt before. But she was fine with it. Soon she came to her senses, floating back down to reality.

"What about you? Don't you—"

His voice was low and as steamy as the hot springs

pool. "I liked watching you. Besides, protection would be a little dicey in here."

Reflexively, she glanced over to the blanket.

But he caressed her cheek. "There's time, Sara. We were discussing the past tonight. I think we'll both know when we're ready to move beyond that."

When he kissed her again, she knew she wanted to move beyond that now. Because she was falling in love with Jase Cramer whether she wanted to or not.

## Chapter Ten

As Jase drove Sara back to the cottage, he thought about the past couple of hours, especially their time in the hot springs pool. He'd come here today fully intending to have sex with her. After all, hadn't she given him the message that she was ready?

However, he found himself putting the brakes on for a couple of reasons. Whether she knew it or not, she was vulnerable. Yes, it had been more than a year since her husband had died, and maybe she was ready to move on from her marriage. On the other hand, she'd just gone through another traumatic event: the fire. She herself had said she'd felt alone after her parents had died and she'd turned to Conrad for that reason. He didn't want her turning to *him* for that reason.

Jase didn't want a woman to turn to him for any reason other than for himself. If that was selfish, so be it. But one failed engagement was enough to make him cautious.

They'd made out in the pool after he'd pleasured her. They'd enjoyed strawberries with cheese and bread along with their water, and he could have easily pleasured them both this time. But after her reaction to his touch, after the almost innocent look in her eyes, he'd felt unsettled... turmoiled...in a way he'd never been before. Maybe he hadn't given in to lust because he was concerned *he'd* be vulnerable, too.

He was glad they couldn't talk easily above the noise of the four-wheeler's engine on the drive back, but as they neared the cottage, he slowed. He didn't want to just drop her off and wave, and that would be it.

So he said, "Let's park this in the shed and I'll walk you over."

The sun was setting now and in the shadows he wasn't sure what he saw on Sara's face. Eagerness to spend more time with him? Or simply joy in returning to her daughter? A child was involved in all of this, so he couldn't make a mistake.

He parked in one of the outbuildings beside a hydraulic auger. After he switched off the ignition, they both climbed out.

He swung his arm around her shoulders. "Do you think Amy's in bed yet?"

"That depends. She might have conned Marissa into a game or two past her bedtime. Jordan could still be toddling around, too. Marissa said he could fall asleep anywhere, but when two kids get together..." She let her voice trail off, the implication clear. "Don't you want to take the cooler and the blankets?"

"I'll get them later. I usually do a final check of the winery just to make sure everything's secure for the night."

Outside, with the night air cooling, she waved her hand at the vineyard. "Being general manager means you're the overseer, doesn't it? Your dad's handed that responsibility down to you."

"I don't know about handed down. He could take over again if he needed to, or hire someone else to do it."

"I doubt he wants to do that. You're his heir."

Jase stared out over the trellises, farther than the eye could see. Maybe it was time to come clean with Sara, to tell her the type of childhood he'd had before he'd come here.

"My father never tells anyone where I really came from."

Shadows played on her face as she responded, "I don't understand. You said he adopted you from the foster care system."

"Yes, he did. I was orphaned at age six and shuffled there from foster home to foster home until I moved in here at twelve. But the real truth is, my mother led a seedy life. She didn't know who my dad was and she died of a drug overdose."

Sara's reaction was immediate. "Jase, I'm so sorry."

"My father likes to brush that part of my history under the rug."

"Maybe he doesn't bring it up because he thinks it's painful for you."

Had Jase even considered that?

"Could it be that you're the one who's ashamed of it, and you constantly try to make good because of it?" she asked perceptively.

"You don't know what you're talking about."

"Maybe not, but I think you want to succeed because at one time no one thought you could."

"Playing the therapist again?"

"You brought this up, Jase, and I'm trying to figure out why. Why tonight, when we got closer?"

*Had* they gotten closer? With Sara, physical intimacy seemed to lead to emotional intimacy. That had never been true with Dana.

They started walking again and as they neared the cottage, Sara suddenly stood her ground and straightened her shoulders. "Do you think you were protecting me tonight—against knowing my own mind and making my own mistakes?"

"Yes, I was protecting you. Your life is unsettled and I don't want to take advantage of you."

"I think that's hogwash. I think you were protecting yourself. Your walls are higher than mine."

When he didn't respond, she turned to go.

The door to the cottage was only about ten yards away, and he *could* just let her fade into her life with Amy without saying another word. But he couldn't let her go like that.

He grabbed her hand, pulled her close and kissed her.

When they broke apart, he didn't have to say anything and neither did she. Words were irrelevant. They wanted each other, maybe even needed each other. Still, he wasn't ready to give in to that need, even if she was.

He would make no mistake this time.

The following day, Jase was working on the next Mommy Club article, going over his interview with Sara. It was going to be a good piece. It would capture readers' attentions and definitely draw them in.

When Liam came into his office for a planned meeting, Jase checked his watch and saw the afternoon had almost disappeared.

"More PR to take along to San Jose to the Wine Expo?" Liam asked with a brow arched.

"No, it's an article for the newspaper."

"Another Mommy Club piece?"

Jase nodded.

"Did Sara give you the go-ahead for her interview to go into print?"

Jase didn't show his surprise that Liam knew about both the article and Sara's interview. "She talked to you about it?" he asked evenly.

"She was unsure about going ahead with it. I just pointed out it would be better for her to lay out the truth rather than letting the general public create fiction. I think I finally persuaded her. I'm glad to see she's taking my advice."

"What specific advice was that?" The fact that Sara had talked this out with Liam rather than him bothered him.

"I told her the truth never hurts. People are going to think what they want, but she should at least give them a fair shot at thinking the right thing."

"So you and Sara are getting to know each other?"

Liam shrugged. "We are. Little by little."

Although Jase wanted to know exactly what that meant, his pride kept him from asking. He wouldn't give Liam the satisfaction of thinking any involvement he had with Sara bothered him.

As Jase studied Liam, he wondered if Sara asked his advice because she liked him…because she trusted his judgment. She didn't know him well enough for that, did she? Or was she attracted to Liam for the same reason she'd been attracted to Conrad—because he was older?

An hour later, his conversation with Liam still running around in his head after their meeting, Jase sat at his desk to do one last edit on the article. When the phone rang, he picked it up automatically. Marissa was long gone.

Checking caller ID, he saw that it was Sara.

After his hello, she said, "I'm so glad you're still there."

"You have my cell number."

"I called that first but got voice mail."

He'd forgotten he'd turned off his phone for his meeting with Liam. "I turned it off for a meeting. What's up?" There was something in her voice that put him on alert. Shakiness? Fearfulness? Something.

"It's Amy. I don't know what to do. She's gone."

"What do you mean *gone*? How's that possible?"

"I had a phone call and when I turned around, she wasn't here. The door wasn't latched properly and I think she went outside. I looked all around, but I don't know which way to go."

"She can't have gone that far. I'll alert everyone and we'll start a search. Stay put. I'll be over there as soon as I call Liam and Dad. If anyone's still left in the winery, they can search, too."

"I can't stay here, Jase. I have to look for her."

He could understand her panic and her need to do something. However—

"What if Amy comes back and you're not there? Then what? Stay put, Sara. Check all around the cottage again, but stay around your place. I'll be there as soon as I can."

Minutes later, Jase's own heart was racing after he made the phone calls. Some winery staff were still working late. Liam had said he'd passed the cleaning crew headed for the reception hall and wine tasting room. He'd round them up.

On his electronic tablet, Jase quickly brought up a map of the winery, divided it into grids and had a plan by the time he arrived at the cottage.

Everyone who was going to help in the search gathered around. Jase saw Liam go to Sara and give her elbow a quick squeeze in reassurance. Maybe the two of them were closer than he thought, but she'd never mentioned it.

Jase quickly divided the search volunteers into groups

and told them how to spread out. Then he said to Sara, "I'm taking the Merlot vineyard. Stay here and wait. Everyone has your cell phone number. As soon as one of us finds her, we'll call you."

"But, Jase, what if—"

The sun was descending lower on the horizon and he knew her fears. "If we don't find her in half an hour, I'll call the sheriff. I promise."

Then, instead of giving her arm a squeeze, he pulled her into a tight hug. "She can't have gone that far," he said again, and kissed the top of Sara's head.

She looked around and spotted his father watching. Jase really didn't care. No time for pretense here.

After giving further instructions to everyone, Jase walked away from Sara but couldn't help looking back over his shoulder. He hadn't seen that pain on her face the night of the fire when she'd appeared on the nightly news. This was her daughter who was lost, not a photo album, not material possessions. His own stomach roiled and his chest was tight. Amy meant a lot to him, too.

Ethan strode toward the Cabernet Sauvignon vineyard behind the cottage, according to Jase's strategy, while Jase headed west and spotted Liam to the south, others heading north. He'd told them to watch for a flash of red—the color of the T-shirt Amy was wearing. He'd also instructed them to look low to the ground in case she'd be in a crouch, peering at a rock or an interesting bug. Amy wasn't afraid of bugs. She was curious about everything.

The trellises, the vines, the rows were all impediments to seeing a small child in an expansive area. Jase listened for laughter. He listened for crying. All he heard was evening birdsong.

He walked. He searched. He thought about calling the sheriff. The weight on his chest made breathing tough. He could only imagine what Sara was feeling. Jase's phone was in his hand and when it rang, he froze. He saw Liam's number.

"Did you find her?"

"Jase, there's nothing out here. We don't know what we're looking for. You need to call the authorities."

"You're looking for red. You're looking for reddish-brown hair. You're looking for a child who could not have gone that far."

"Maybe you want to be the hero here, but you've got to be practical."

Did he want to be Sara's hero? Sure, why not. After all, he was getting in deeper. But more than anything else, he just wanted to find a little girl who'd crawled into his heart.

"Ten more minutes, Liam, then I'll call. Search low and search behind."

As each second ticked by, Jase's optimism fled. What did he know about searching? What did he know about relationships? What did he know about finding one lost little girl?

The next time Jase's phone buzzed, his father's number flashed on the screen. He suspected Ethan was going to give him the same advice as Liam had. Instead, however, Ethan's voice was jubilant.

"I found her! Something about she saw a cat and she chased after it."

There were a couple of cats at the winery. Liam had taken them to the vet now and then, and he kept a stash of cat food in the storage cupboard.

"Did you call Sara?" Jase asked.

"I thought you'd like to do that. Meet you at her place."

Jase could hear Amy in the background, and the gentleness in his father's voice when Ethan said to her, "I'll take you home to your mommy. Come on, now." Then he clicked off.

Jase wondered about that gentleness…wondered how his father would be with a grandchild.

Grandchild? What was he thinking of?

He jogged back to Sara's cottage, on the phone the whole way, alerting Sara her daughter had been found, alerting the searchers they could come home.

Sara ran toward Ethan and Amy as they came into view. When Jase had phoned her to tell her his father had found her daughter, her legs had almost buckled. Now she rushed toward them, eager to see Amy and make sure she was okay. However, the sight of them made her stop. Ethan looked like a grandfather, holding his granddaughter's hand. He had his head bent low and was speaking to her. Sara wondered what he was saying.

Moving again, Sara reached Amy and hugged her tight. "I lost you and couldn't find you! Where did you go?"

"Kitty ran off and I went, too."

Sara crouched before Amy. "Honey, look at me."

Amy did.

"Don't ever go outside without my permission…or without *me.* It's a great big world and I don't want you to get lost. If Mr. Cramer hadn't found you, it would have gotten dark and you would have been out here all alone. Promise me you won't do that again."

Amy's eyes grew really big and her lower lip quivered. "Are you mad?"

Sara gave her another hug. "No, I'm not mad. I was just very, very worried. Can you promise you won't go out without me?"

"I promise," she said solemnly.

Standing, Sara faced Ethan. "Thank you. I don't know how to express how much your search meant."

Ethan's expression was gentle. "I understand how a parent feels when a child is lost. When Jase was thirteen, he disappeared and we couldn't find him."

Jase's voice came from behind her. "I don't remember that."

"We found you reading a book in the springhouse."

Sara saw a shadow pass over Jase's face as he must have suddenly remembered exactly why he'd been in the springhouse. "I wasn't trying to run away."

"No, maybe not, but you were trying to find a place where you felt you belonged."

Jase's face showed surprise at his father's perception. He went silent until he glanced at Amy. "You had quite an adventure. I think we have sweet rolls at the house. Interested?"

Amy looked up at Sara for permission.

"That sounds good," Sara agreed. "We'll get a bath, and then we'll have a snack." She noticed all the volunteers had left, returning to whatever they were doing before Jase's call had summoned them. Liam, too. She'd make a point of thanking everyone personally.

An hour later, Amy smelled of strawberry shampoo when Jase arrived with the sweet rolls. Amy grinned at him, oblivious of the chaos she'd caused as her fingers became sticky with icing, and grape filling smudged her upper lip.

"You'll need another bath," Jase teased her. Then he said to Sara, "Watching her enjoy a sweet roll has got to be one of your best visual memories. I should have brought my camera."

Sara thought about the other photos he'd taken. She'd

framed them, placing them around the cottage. He'd given her more that he'd taken at the wine and music festival.

"Speaking of memories," she said, "I can't quite imagine you running away and holing up in the springhouse with a book."

"I'd forgotten about that one. I'm surprised my dad remembered it."

"I'll bet he remembers more than you give him credit for."

"I was pretty defensive back then. Sullen, too."

"I can understand that."

"I don't think my dad could. He expected me to be thankful for being adopted and just fit in somehow. I wish it had been that easy."

"But you did fit in eventually."

"I did. But by then it was as if he and I had this great divide between us. We've never been able to bridge it."

"I hope that never happens between me and Amy."

"It won't. You'll make sure it doesn't."

"Even when the teenage hormones surge?"

"You'll need a gatekeeper to turn the boys away."

She could imagine Jase being that gatekeeper.

Seeing Amy was finished with her sweet roll, Sara said, "Let's get you washed up again and into bed."

"Can Jase say prayers with me?"

Saying prayers was different from reading a story and she didn't know how Jase would feel about that. When she glanced at him, she saw he looked surprised.

"You don't have to," she assured him quickly.

Instead of answering Sara, he focused on Amy. "I hope you're good at saying prayers because I'm not. Maybe you can show me how."

"Okay," Amy said as if it were no big deal.

So that's how, ten minutes later, they were gathered in

Amy's room, Jase sitting on her bed with her. "How does this go?" Jase asked.

"I tell God what I'm thankful for."

"And what are you thankful for?"

Amy folded her hands and closed her eyes. "I'm thankful for our new house and for Mommy and Jordan and Marissa and you." Opening her eyes, she said in a low voice to Jase, "Then I ask God to bless everyone."

"Okay," Jase agreed.

"God bless Mommy and Jordan and Marissa and you and Mr. Cramer, too. He found me. And bless kitty cat."

She unfolded her hands and opened her eyes. "That's it."

"You did a good job." Jase couldn't hide the smile in his voice.

"That's what Mommy says."

"And now Mommy says it's time for sleep." Sara stood and so did Jase. She could see he didn't know whether to stay or go.

She pulled the sheet up to Amy's neck and kissed her forehead. "Good night, little one. Have very sweet dreams."

Jase bent to Amy, laid his hand on her hair and then moved away. Sara wondered what he was thinking as they returned to the living room.

She didn't have to wonder for long as he said, "I hope she takes her time growing up."

"I know what you mean." When they reached the sofa, Sara suggested, "I think Amy and your dad bonded."

"I didn't get the feeling that he scolded her for running away," Jase agreed, looking pensive.

"Did he scold you when you ran away?"

After a thoughtful pause, Jase shook his head. "No, he didn't, come to think of it. He asked me about the book I was reading. It was *Treasure Island* and he said he'd read it as a boy. I'd forgotten all about that conversation."

"Sometimes it's not so bad taking a stroll down memory lane."

"No, sometimes it's not." He took her into his arms, then, and gave her one of those long, wet kisses that made her want to strip his clothes off and hers, too.

After he raised his head, his expression showing he didn't want to stop any more than she did, he told her, "I'm going to a wine expo in San Jose next weekend. It's just an overnight trip. I'll leave Saturday morning, be back by Sunday evening. How would you like to come along?"

Late afternoon on Wednesday, Sara stood beside Ramona at the Four Oaks Ranch, watching Connie Russo on a bay as she led two children on their own horses around the ring. Sara had decided to introduce Ramona to Connie because she thought it might help her attitude.

Ramona said, "They look like they're having a lot of fun."

"They are. Connie says the lessons teach them confidence, balance and independence."

An SUV had driven up while they were talking and a young woman who looked to be in her thirties climbed out. She walked over to Sara and Ramona and motioned to the ring.

"Those are my two."

"They're doing great," Ramona noted. "Good seats and handling the reins well."

"Do you help out here?" the woman asked.

"No, I don't," Ramona said.

Sara was hoping Ramona would want to. Soon Ramona would be able to ride again. Maybe not out on the trail, but here in the ring. She could give her input from the ground for now and Connie could use the help.

The two children dismounted and the mom excused

herself to go get them. They all climbed into the SUV and drove off.

Connie joined Sara and Ramona at the fence, extending her hand to Ramona.

"It's good to meet you. Sara told me you used to ride a lot."

"I took tourists on trail rides up into the mountains, did a lot of camping on my own, too. But then I was in a biking accident and everything changed. I haven't been on a horse in six months."

"Do you think you're good to ride now?"

Ramona glanced at Sara. "I guess that's up to Sara. I feel stronger than I did since I've been working with her, but my leg muscles are still weaker than I'd like."

"Riding will help strengthen them again, you know that," Connie told her.

"Yes, I do. I guess I'm just scared."

"We all fear whatever might hurt us," Connie said.

That sentence hit home with Sara. When Jase had asked her to go along to the expo in San Jose, she hadn't given him an answer. She'd told him she'd think about it, that she would have to see about someone watching Amy. She'd also said she wasn't sure being separated from Amy was a good thing right now. But the real reason for her hesitation was fear. If she went with Jase, she knew she'd be intimate with him, and she wasn't sure where that was going to lead.

For the moment, however, she had to put thoughts of San Jose aside to focus on Ramona. "I think it would do you good to be out in the sun, to just be around horses again and to feel your way. You're strong enough to get back in the saddle on a gentle horse, but you have to *feel* you're ready."

"Oh, I have a couple of gentle ones," Connie assured them. "It will feel like being in a rocking chair when you ride them. One's a quarter horse and only fourteen hands high, so you wouldn't be that far off the ground, either. But as Sara said, you have to feel ready. You could start by watching some lessons, telling me how you think the kids are handling their horses, nothing strenuous, nothing threatening for anyone."

"How often would you like me to help?" Ramona asked, almost looking eager.

"How about a couple of mornings a week? Then over lunch we could discuss how you feel and what you saw with the kids."

"I think that sounds like a good start," Ramona said, and she turned to Sara. "Thank you."

"No thanks necessary. And we'll keep working on strengthening your arms and legs plus your stamina. That treadmill and stair stepper is just waiting for you."

Ramona laughed and it was the first genuine laugh Sara had heard since she'd begun treating her. Facing fear was probably the best way to face life.

So...could she face her doubts and fears and go along with Jase to San Jose?

First she'd talk to Kaitlyn and see if she could watch Amy overnight. If that could be arranged, then she'd call Jase. She'd tell him she'd go to the wine expo with him and find out if he was going to reserve two rooms...or one.

## Chapter Eleven

Sara could hardly keep her eyes off of Jase as he drove to San Jose—his strong hands on the wheel, the breadth of his shoulders, the way his expression changed when he talked to her or watched the road.

But there was tension between them that was her fault. She knew he wanted to ease it when he said, "Tell me why you don't want anyone to know you're in San Jose with me."

"Marissa and Kaitlyn know." When Jase had come to the cottage to pick her up, she'd given Kaitlyn last-minute details and asked her not to tell anyone about her trip with Jase unless absolutely necessary.

"And my father," he added. "But I don't understand why it's a secret from anyone else."

"With my interview running in the paper on Monday, I don't want to start more gossip."

"You don't want anyone to think we're having an affair?"

They weren't. Yet.

When she didn't respond, he glanced at her. "I told you the suite has two bedrooms. This trip can be whatever you want it to be."

She knew what she wanted it to be. But risking her heart again would take courage. Unless she could just look at this weekend as the start of an affair and nothing more.

But could she ever just have an affair with Jase?

She doubted it. If she made love with him, she'd be risking her heart, taking a chance on love again.

That thought was scary, almost as scary as something else she needed to tell him. "I got a call from Mr. Kiplinger's secretary while I was packing."

Jase cast her a considering glance. "Has the insurance company made a determination?"

"I don't know. She wouldn't tell me what High Point decided, just that I needed to make an appointment with Mr. Kiplinger. He was out of town, so we set it up for Friday. I can use a personal day."

"No hint of their decision?"

"No. But I think I'll try to call him myself on Monday."

"He's not going to tell you anything before he has to."

"I know. But it won't hurt to call."

"You persevere, don't you?"

"What other choice is there?"

"Lots of people give up."

"*You* didn't."

"No. Because of you." He reached over and took her hand.

She liked holding Jase's hand. She liked the idea of doing it for a very long time.

Two hours later, the bellhop opened the door into the

executive suite and returned Jase's key card to him. The hotel was attached to the convention center where the wine expo was being held. The lobby had been luxuriously modern, and now she saw that the sitting area of the suite was, also, decorated in plush claret and soothing gray. But what attracted Sara most were the panoramic views of the cityscape.

After the bellhop deposited their suitcases in the bedrooms—one in each—Jase tipped him and closed the door. "What do you think?"

Still entranced by the view, she responded, "It's a world away from the vineyard."

Jase came up behind her at the floor-to-ceiling windows. "Yes, it is."

He was so close, she could feel his body heat. She *did* want to be close to him. She leaned back against him and thought again about tonight. Separate bedrooms? Or should she let her desire and feelings for him win out over her fears? His arms came around her and they stood looking out at the city. She could feel his heat, his energy, his passion.

She'd turned into his arms, ready for his kiss, when his cell phone beeped.

"I'll let it go to voice mail," he muttered.

She'd come along knowing this was a business trip for him. "Didn't you say you were expecting calls from other vintners who would be here?"

"Do you always have to be so practical?"

"As a mom, I have to be practical."

Bestowing a quick kiss on her lips anyway, he shook his head and took his phone from his belt. When he glanced at the number, he frowned.

"Do you need privacy?" she asked.

"It's my editor," he said in a low voice. "Rather, he *was* my editor a long time ago."

Jase answered the call with, "Hi, Matt. It's been a long time."

After a few moments, Jase glanced at Sara. "So you heard about the article."

Uneasy, Sara suspected what was coming next. If Jase's editor knew Jase was writing again, photographing again—some of his photos of the food collection for the summer lunch program had been in the paper and online—he might want him to write something in particular, something that could take Jase across the world.

Fidgety now, she crossed to the desk on the pretense of examining the room-service menu. Paging through it, she was far enough away from Jase that she didn't hear most of the conversation.

She'd gone through the service directory, the restaurant menu, the concierge services and all the other amenities that were available by the time Jase ended the call.

"Important?" she asked lightly.

He looked serious when he responded, "Possibly."

"Do you want to talk about it?"

"I have to think about it. In September, Matt wants me to fly to Africa with a group of doctors who are setting up a clinic."

"Is the area dangerous?"

"Any area there is dangerous. On a scale of one to ten, this is about a five. There's a need for the doctors and a need for the word to get out about the conditions there. I'd be an asset since I can document the trip in photos and by blogging."

"Like what you did before."

"Yes. But the time frame would be limited. I'd only be there about a week until they got the clinic set up. He also has another junket planned for November. But that story is in Alabama. It's about kids again, conditions in the schools…and literacy in general. Both are great opportunities to help."

"You could do a lot of good," she agreed, though she didn't want to. If Jase took up his former life, where would that leave her and Amy?

"It's a lot to think about," he said, watching her.

"Yes, it is. Could Ethan spare you for that long?"

"I'm not sure. Liam and Tony might be able to take over for a week or so."

The romantic mood had definitely been broken. All of her doubts about seriously getting involved with Jase had resurfaced. Now he would be preoccupied with a decision he had to make. "How soon do you have to let him know?"

"By July fifteenth."

She was under no illusions that Jase would turn down these assignments. Photojournalism and good causes were in his blood. Her throat felt tight and tears weren't far away. She swallowed, took a deep breath and said, "I'd better unpack or my dress for dinner will need more than a little steaming." She'd brought along the dress she'd worn for the soiree, as well as a plain black one that could suit any occasion. Though fashion was the last thing she wanted to think about right now.

"After you unpack, do you want to come with me to the wine expo for a while?"

That was the reason Jase was here. And she'd come along to be with him. Time sampling wine could give them breathing room for the decisions they both had to make.

Jase knew so many people at the expo, from the sommeliers to the representatives from the vineyards and the cellars. There was a thread of restrained tension between her and Jase, and Sara knew that had come from his phone conversation. She didn't know how he really felt about her and how she fit into his future. *If* she fit into his future. And he didn't know how she felt about him...how she'd fallen for him in a huge way. Was he really thinking about going back to a life of travel, writing and photography? Would he actually leave the vineyard behind?

Each time he glanced at her, she knew the questions were in her eyes. She knew he could read the anxiety on her face. She knew he was already making up his mind. She'd come to realize Jase was a decisive person and decisions wouldn't wait.

As they stood at a high table sampling a Chardonnay Jase had chosen and snacking on an assortment of cheeses and crackers, a gray-haired man stopped and shook Jase's hand.

Jase introduced him to Sara. "Travis Goodman, this is Sara Stevens. Sara, Travis makes superior wine at Valley Vineyards."

After a nod to Sara, the older man asked Jase, "So are you speaking at the symposium in January?"

"I haven't decided yet."

"You'd have a lot to offer."

"Liam is talking about organic processes."

"I know. And so are other winemakers. But general management is an area that's changing year by year. We'd all like to hear how you're rolling with the changes."

Jase laughed. "You want me to give away all our secrets."

"Maybe not *all*. Just some. Your wine club has a reputation for being one of the best."

"That secret is easy. We give away freebies and coupons."

"Yes, but patrons have to *want* to participate in the vineyard's activities. They have to *want* to buy your wines. And they do."

"Raintree is more than a brand. It's a way of life. We have a history behind us."

"Yes, you do. Your father's been around the block a few times and he learned it from his dad. I'm glad you're continuing in the tradition. That has to be important to Ethan." He smiled at Sara. "I'll let you enjoy your Chardonnay from a cellar other than ours. Don't forget to stop by Valley's table."

"We won't. I have to keep up with my competition," Jase assured him.

Jase was joking. But Sara could see something different in his expression since Travis had mentioned Ethan. Would Jase talk about it here in the midst of chatter and noise, wine pouring and an all-around celebratory atmosphere?

She leaned closer to him so he could hear her. "What's the symposium Travis spoke about?"

"It's an event that brings together winemakers, labelers, distributors, even bottle vendors...everyone involved in the wine-making industry from all over the world."

"How's it different from this?"

"Oh, it's much different. It's more of a conference atmosphere. And like a trade show. It's usually in Sacramento in January."

"So you'd be giving a workshop?"

"If I decide to do it. As I told Travis, Liam is giving one. I'd be taking Dad's place."

"So he wants you to do it?"

"Oh, yes. He hates all the schmoozing now."

"You can talk to anyone about anything."

"Is this going somewhere?"

Yes, it was, though Sara knew this was the part Jase

might not want to talk about. "If you fly off to Africa again, how's that going to affect Ethan?"

Studying his wineglass, he turned it slowly. "I've been thinking about that, but I don't have an answer. I do know he thinks Raintree is the be-all and end-all of the world. I don't."

It was easy to hear the certainty in his voice and she knew what that meant. "So you've made up your mind."

"I've made up my mind about doing the article on the doctors' clinic…and doing the project in Alabama. My father and I will just have to figure out who can take up the slack while I'm gone."

"What if he doesn't want you to go?" In her mind she was thinking, *What if I don't want you to go?*

"I already know he won't want me to go. But I have to do what I feel is right, not what he thinks is safe."

And that went for her, too. She could see it in Jase's gaze…in his body language…in his attitude.

Sara watched Jase pick up his wineglass, saw him take a swallow. His hand made the glass look fragile and small. She remembered all too well what his touch felt like. Just thinking about it stoked the familiar heat inside her. Making love with Jase would be the biggest risk of her life. She'd be starting an affair, and she'd never had an affair. Maybe some women would find that exciting and dream-fulfilling, but her dreams had always been about a family, about a husband she could count on, about a life filled with commitment and promises. If Jase flew off at a moment's notice, how could they have commitment and promises? If he was in and out of her life, how would that affect Amy?

Jase suddenly leaned toward her, wrapped his arm around her shoulders and murmured against her temple, "You're thinking too much. Let's just enjoy the time we have here."

She hadn't practiced a lot of living in the moment. Could Jase teach her how to do it? As a mom, could she do it?

When she didn't respond, he said, "Let's go upstairs and get ready for dinner. I know a great restaurant with global cuisine that you might like."

All his offer did was make her think again about Jase leaving. He had been around the globe, sampling all kinds of foods, and he wanted to do it again.

As they walked through the hotel lobby, she noted the guests coming and going, wheeling suitcases, carrying duffel bags and leather briefcases. Men in expensive suits carried laptops or sat working on them in the leather club chairs. Jase was part of this world. She imagined his suit was custom-tailored, too. Although Jase had been in hotel lobbies like this all over the world, she knew he'd also lived under the most dangerous conditions. He'd been shot at and almost died.

On the other hand, she'd never left California. Before she'd met Conrad, she hadn't had the opportunity or the funds. Afterward, she was focused on her marriage and then a baby. Now Amy was her life.

She had to figure out how Jase fit in that life. *If* he fit in. If who she was when she was with him was better than who she was when she was alone.

In the elevator, they didn't speak. She felt Jase glance at her now and then, but she wasn't sure what her response would be if their gazes met. She wasn't sure about anything. Her stomach felt turned upside down. And she felt turned inside out.

In the suite, they went to their separate rooms to get ready, and she wondered what they were going to talk about over dinner...just how honest they could be.

In her room, she stared at the two dresses she'd brought along—the Carzanne and the black sheath. She hadn't asked Jase how dressy this restaurant was. Maybe she should ask him which one would be more appropriate. She didn't want to stand out like the proverbial sore thumb.

Sara was intent on getting an answer to her question as she saw Jase's partially opened bedroom door and rapped on it. A second later, he was standing there in front of her, shirtless and beltless and his dress slacks were undone at the waist. Touching him in the hot springs pool vividly clicked through her mind. Every sensation she'd felt that day was alive in her once more. Desire burned in her belly and her feelings for him threatened to break loose.

"You've seen me dressed in less than this," he said with a twist of a smile.

Yes, she had. But this seemed different somehow. They were alone…in a hotel suite. And she'd come on this trip because—

Because she'd fallen in love with him.

"Sara?" he asked as she stared at his chest and the whirling black hair and the dip of his slacks under his navel.

"I—" She moistened very dry lips. "I wondered how dressed up to get for tonight. If I should wear the Carzanne or something simpler." Her gaze lifted to his and locked on his sensual gray eyes.

"Anything goes. It's up to you what you want to wear."

Yes, it seemed *everything* was up to her.

"Sara?" He was looking as if he wanted to take her into his arms. She felt foolish, now, naive and gauche, as if she'd never been anywhere and he'd been everywhere. She was scared she'd make a mess of her feelings for Jase…of her happiness and Amy's.

"I'll be ready in about twenty minutes," she said, and started to turn away. But he clasped her shoulder before she could, and the heat of his hand through her silky blouse was scorching.

His voice was deep and husky, indicating he was in some turmoil as he said, "I know you're upset about my decision to take the assignment in Africa."

"I'm not upset," she said with a shake of her head. "Just unsure…about where *we're* going."

He brought her a little closer. "Not everything has to be about the future. Maybe we just need to take one step at a time. You're here with me. I want to be with you. Really *be* with you. Isn't that enough?"

She closed her eyes for a moment. He was right, wasn't he? Couldn't her life be about more than planning ahead? More than being a mom? More than about the constant fear she was making the wrong decisions? It could simply be about her love for Jase.

Gazing up at him, so close that the tips of her breasts touched his chest, she knew this was a now or never moment. She and Jase could eke out such little time alone. She wasn't going to waste tonight on doubts and worries and maybes. She wanted to focus on feelings and desires. Hers for him and his for her.

"For once in my life, I want to grab the moment." She felt breathless with the thought of it.

Jase's slow smile turned up his lips, and then he swept her up into his arms. Kissing her all the way, he held her close and carried her to the king-sized bed.

When he broke the kiss, he stared down at her with so much desire she thought she'd melt.

"I want this," she told Jase so he'd have no doubts.

"When you asked me what you should wear tonight, I wanted to say, 'Nothing.'"

"That might raise a few eyebrows."

"It would raise more than eyebrows!"

After kissing her again, he let her feet drop to the side of the bed. One arm still around her, he took hold of the comforter and sheets and threw them back in one swoop. That huge surface with its pristine taupe sheet said it all. They were going to make love there. *She* was going to make love there. Maybe soon she'd know what Jase felt, too. Maybe afterward, though their worlds would be different, they could find a way to make them overlap.

Jase's fingers went to the buttons on her blouse. One by one he opened them, letting his finger drag along her skin as he did. He was creating excitement...and need... and longing for something she'd never had—a man who desired her as much as she desired him.

As Jase's fingers fumbled a bit, she realized he wasn't as cool as he pretended to be. He gave her a half smile and a shrug.

After he'd unfastened the last button, she reached out and touched the hair on his chest. She followed the swirls in a glide down to his navel and, to her delight, he sucked in a breath.

He shook his head. "It would take me about a minute to tear your clothes off you and ravish you on that bed. But I want to give us both more pleasure than that."

"We have all night," she said softly, and it was a promise.

Her words seemed to unwrap his control. He unfastened her bra, unhooked the clasp at her waist and stripped off her slacks.

"Too fast?" he asked, looking down at her, slipping his hands under the elastic of her panties and clasping her backside. When he pulled her flush against him, she was already wishing *he* was naked, too. "Not too fast. Not too slow. Just right." She was trying to flirt with him, to keep up the banter, to hide the intensity of the love and passion swirling inside her.

He laughed, scooped her up again and laid her on the

bed. Then he stripped quickly and joined her, as if he was afraid she'd disappear if he looked away too long.

"I want to do everything with you," he said in a deep husky voice that thrilled her.

Her sex life with Conrad had been very traditional. She wasn't sure what "everything" was, but she was looking forward to trying it with Jase. "What do you have in mind?" she asked, realizing that flirting with him was easy. So why was it so hard to tell him what she was feeling?

"Why don't I start by kissing you all over?"

When he began at her forehead and tenderly stroked her hair, she felt ridiculously like crying. He trailed kisses down her cheek and took her mouth with a deeply erotic search without giving her a chance to even touch him. Stringing kisses to her earlobe, he teased it with his tongue until she restlessly moved on the sheets.

She did reach for him then, but he just chuckled, took both of her hands and held them above her head. "I'll let you have some fun next time. Let me have mine now."

Fun? He called this fun? He was sensually torturing her. And she loved every kiss, every stroke of his tongue, every brush of his fingers. He definitely knew how to please a woman, but she kicked that thought out of her head. She wouldn't wander into his romantic past. Not tonight, when everything was just for the two of them.

As he held one hand on either side of her head and dipped lower to her breast, she felt more excited than she'd ever believed she could.

"I *am* going to touch you," he warned. "All over."

His gaze held hers and he could tell she enjoyed the idea of what he was proposing. Finally she let his hands go so he could move lower and lower and lower.

"Jase, you're not—"

"I said all over."

Yes, he had, and she knew what he was about to do would make her feel more vulnerable than she'd felt before. Could she trust him that much? Could she trust herself to believe in a future with him no matter where he wandered?

When he spread her thighs with his hands, she felt the roughened calluses. The sensation of rough against smooth had her reaching for his shoulders. His tongue swirled where she least expected to be kissed...where she felt more sensations than anyplace else on her body. As he teased and taunted, she dug her fingers into the thick and vibrantly silky hair that she loved touching.

"Jase, you're going to make me come apart again." She remembered the last time and how he had guarded not only his feelings but his physical needs. She took a deep breath and tried to gather her thoughts. "You can't just shut down tonight. You can't just tell me you want *my* pleasure. Not this time."

A beat of silence filled the room until he agreed solemnly, "Not this time."

Those words made her even wilder with wanting as his tongue circled her center, as he slid one finger inside of her, then two...as he found the spot that could unravel her.

Her ears began to buzz and she realized she was panting. "I don't want to have a climax without you."

The words were out of her mouth before she could stop them, making herself explicitly clear.

"You can have one, and then another. I'll prove it to you."

He was so sure of her body when she wasn't. He must have some magic formula, some magic touch. That was exactly what it turned out to be. She'd never felt as if she was the center of someone's universe before as she felt it with Jase. As she allowed him the intimate pleasure of bringing her to climax with his mouth, she hung on to him, scraped her nails down his back, called his name, hoping the walls in these suites were soundproof. Her body had been wound tightly, but now in the extreme pleasure, all tension fled.

But emotion didn't. Love for Jase welled up, overtaking her, finally bringing those tears to her eyes.

He saw them and gently swiped one away. But then he didn't give her time for the afterglow to fade. Reaching to the nightstand, he pulled a condom from the drawer and rolled it on. Rising above her, he again held her hands above her shoulders and entered her with a smooth, slick thrust. At the same time, he entwined their fingers, a symbolic gesture that touched her soul.

She didn't believe she could feel any more. She'd never had a double orgasm. Why would she expect one now? But Jase had other ideas. He wasn't even questioning the possibility. He slid in and out, slowly at first so she got used to him…used to the idea of being filled by him. But then he thrust harder and she held on tighter and the world rocked and seemed to break apart into thousands of sparkling pieces. She urged him on by rocking her body hard against his, by arching up to meet his thrusts, by wanting everything he would give.

At this moment as her world burst around her, she let go of fear and held on to only hope. Jase's release came after her orgasm, sending the last waves of sensation through her. His deep guttural sigh of pleasure made her feel proud and self-satisfied. She imagined he'd felt that way that night at the hot springs.

But just because he'd made love with her didn't mean he'd open his heart and soul to her. She'd meant what she'd said about having all night, but she didn't know how he'd feel about that. Or if he'd want it, too. She was afraid to depend on desire when what she really wanted and needed was deep trust, abiding love, total commitment.

When he collapsed on top of her, she loved being surrounded by him. She breathed in his male scent and rubbed against the rougher texture of his skin. Neither of them spoke for a few minutes as their breathing returned to normal.

Finally Jase lifted his head.

She kept her arms tightly around him. "You don't have to move," she whispered, loving the feel of them joined together like this.

"I'm too heavy for you."

"You're not."

She felt him move inside her again and smiled.

"Ah, Sara, what you do to me."

"Physically?"

"And in other ways, too."

As they rested in their total communion, she mused, "We're supposed to be getting dressed for dinner."

Lifting his head again, he arched a brow at her. "There *are* other options. We could go out much later. Or...we could order room service. Though I did want to introduce you to global cuisine," he reminded her with a wicked glint in his eye.

She took her arms from around him, and held one hand to her right and one hand to her left. "There are two scales." She lowered her left hand a little. "Global cuisine." Then she lowered her right hand a lot more. "Staying in bed with you. Guess which one wins?"

"So your decision is as easily made as that." He sounded smug.

"No contest at all. Now, if you'd rather eat sushi or chicken cordon bleu—"

He kissed her again, stopping her words efficiently, letting her know staying in bed with her was more important to him, too.

Sara felt Jase's arms around her as she awakened the next morning. Last night had been a dream come true. They'd ordered room service, called Amy to say goodnight, fed each other bits of lobster, then made love long into the night. They hadn't talked much. Just touched and kissed and sighed. She'd been amazed by how the pleasure had grown, expanded, encompassed them both time after time. Their lovemaking hadn't slaked desire but awakened it.

Jase's arms tightened around her and she smiled. Spooned together, she could feel his arousal.

"I see you're awake," she teased.

"Sure am. Just waiting for you."

Turning into his arms, she smiled. "I suppose you don't need much sleep?"

"I can fall asleep in an instant and wake up with the snap of fingers."

He was nuzzling her neck and kissing her ear when her cell phone buzzed.

He gave her one more kiss on the lips and raised his head. "You'd better answer in case it's Kaitlyn."

One of the many things she loved about Jase was his acceptance that her daughter came first.

When she reached for her phone on the nightstand, she saw Kaitlyn's caller ID. But Amy was the one on the line. "Mornin', Mommy. Kaitlyn said I could call."

"Do you miss me?"

"Yep. But you'll be home today, right?"

"Right. Probably around the time you're eating supper."

After a few more minutes of conversation, Kaitlyn came on the line, too, to assure her all was well.

Shortly after, Sara ended the call with a sigh.

"What?" Jase asked, noticing from across the bed.

"Reality crashed in, reminding me I have a life in Fawn Grove. I love it. I love Amy. But I guess it also reminded me I have to call Mr. Kiplinger tomorrow. And Friday—"

Jase levered himself across the bed and sat beside her. "I'm supposed to fly to San Diego on Friday with Tony for meetings. I'll be back Saturday. Do you want me to postpone the trip?"

She loved the fact that he'd do that for her. She loved *him* so much. But that love was new. She felt she had to stand alone with this problem until it was resolved. "Don't postpone your trip. If the company has made a decision, nothing will change it."

After he studied her, he took her into his arms. "Whatever it is, you'll deal with it."

Yes, she would. But if the decision wasn't in her favor—

She couldn't think about that now. She wouldn't think about that now. She had today with Jase, and she was going to enjoy every minute of it.

## Chapter Twelve

Jase pulled his car into the garage attached to the main house and pressed the remote for the garage door. It slid down and he switched off the ignition. Then he glanced at Sara with so many thoughts and feelings swirling inside him that he couldn't make sense of them. If he went out on assignment, what would happen to them? This woman was beginning to be more important than he ever expected.

"Back home," he commented nonchalantly.

She smiled at him, and that smile made his heart ache. "Where reality sets in," she remarked.

He knew what Sara was facing this week with her appointment with Kiplinger, but wondered if there was more to her concern. "Are you worried about your interview being released tomorrow?"

Shifting toward him, she shrugged. "To tell you the truth, I'm more worried about what the insurance investigator will have to say. The interview will either set things straight or it won't. As someone told me, I can't control public opinion."

Was that someone Liam? And why didn't she mention him if he was the one whose advice she'd taken? After what had happened between them this weekend, he sent jealousy packing. "In the long run, public opinion doesn't matter. You're never going to know if your interview was the impetus to make somebody in need pick up the phone and call The Mommy Club."

"I'll be optimistic about that."

"Be optimistic about Kiplinger, too. Hopefully the company found the direct cause of the fire and there won't be any more doubts."

They went quiet for a little while and neither of them seemed eager to exit the car.

Sara asked, "Do you want to come over for a while?"

"I'd like to. But I really should talk to my father and let him know about the trips. We'll have to make some arrangements." He really didn't know how his dad would react. Or maybe he did and he just wanted to get the confrontation over with sooner rather than later.

Except...

When he looked at Sara now, he didn't want to leave her tonight. When he looked at Sara, he wanted her all over again. How crazy was that, after all the time they'd spent in bed? But having sex with her hadn't eased his desire. Having sex with her had made him just want to find satisfaction over and over again.

He exited the car and so did Sara. They closed their doors, opened the back doors and each took their suitcase from the backseat.

When he came around to Sara's side, he dropped his suitcase on the floor. "When are we going to find some time alone again?" he asked, closing in on her because he had to kiss her once more before they parted.

She set her suitcase down, too. "I don't know. After Amy goes to bed, you could come over and—"

"Duck into your bedroom and not make any noise?"

"I don't know if that's possible."

He felt some male satisfaction when she blushed. And when she looked up at him with those big brown eyes, he wrapped his arms around her and kissed her like he'd wanted to kiss her during the endless drive home. At least it had seemed endless. Two and a half hours of being close to her yet not touching her had made him aroused and uncomfortable.

They were alone now and who knew when they'd be alone again? He broke off the kiss, went the few feet to the door and locked it.

"What are you doing?"

"That's the only entrance that can be opened from the outside. I wanted to give us a little privacy."

"You're not seriously considering—"

When he kissed her again, he made sure she knew exactly what he was considering.

This time, she tore away and braced her hands on his chest. "I've never done anything like this."

He heard the excitement in her voice. "There's a first time for everything," he muttered, pressing his body against hers, stroking her hair away from her temple, kissing her neck.

Soon she was plucking at his polo shirt, lifting it from his waist, putting her hands on his skin.

Sara's hands on him was a touch he'd imagined many times. But his imagination hadn't been equal to the reality. In his dreams, she'd come to him when he knew he couldn't have her. Then suddenly yesterday, there she was in his bed, responding wildly to everything he did, passionately returning his hunger. Right now, she was like that again and he couldn't have stopped if the fire department had turned a hose on him. Sara brought him so much pleasure, he almost didn't know himself when he was with her. He felt unfettered by his background, free from his past, healed from an ordeal that had cost him too much. Because of the way she made him need her, he felt walls crumbling, defenses lowering. When he wasn't with her, he felt disconcerted, missing her and Amy, yet avoiding a dream that could hurt too much if it blew up in his face.

It was easier to concentrate on the physical, to give in to the lust, to enjoy the pleasure.

She was wearing a skirt. While he kissed the pulse at her throat, he filled his hands with it, then dragged it up to her waist.

She reached for his belt and fumbled with the buckle. He made quick work of it, grabbed her panties and skimmed them down her legs.

Holding his shoulder, she stepped out of them. After he slid his hand up her inner thigh, he felt her and she was ready. More than ready.

So was he.

Seconds later, he was naked from the waist down, kissing her and lifting her at the same time. He groaned when she wrapped her legs around him. They were leaning against the hood of his car. It was still warm, but it didn't begin to match the heat they were generating. This primitive urge to possess her rattled him as it had this morning…and since the first day he'd met her. He didn't know what the future would bring, but he knew what he wanted right now.

He wanted to bury himself in Sara.

And that's exactly what he did.

Every time she moaned, every time she said, "More, Jase," every time he plunged a little deeper, he felt more satisfied, yet more hungry. Sara's fingers clutched his neck, her nails scraped his backside. He felt changed in some intangible way.

She unraveled first, called his name, clutched him tighter. His world closed in until only this woman and his response to her existed. When his release came it was mind-blowing, and not a single sane thought remained in his head.

With them both still leaning against the hood of the car, her legs slid from around him and he pulled away. She was pulling her skirt down around her when reality, like cold water thrown in his face, jolted his mind and he realized what they'd done.

She must have realized it about the same time because her gaze met his and her hand came up to her mouth. "Oh, my gosh," she said.

"We didn't use protection," he finished for her. He could see the quick calculations in her mind.

"We should be okay."

Now she wasn't looking at him, and he didn't like that at all. He cupped her chin in his hand. "If you're pregnant, I'll stand by you."

She looked confused for a moment as if she wondered what that meant. He wasn't sure himself. But he did know if he had a child, he'd claim it.

She swooped down to the floor and picked up her panties. "I have to get back to Amy."

Yes, she did.

They should talk about what happened. Still, what was the point? What would be, would be.

As soon as Sara entered Raintree's offices with Amy and Jordan on Monday evening, Amy made a beeline for Jase's office, the picture she'd drawn flapping in her hand.

Marissa took Jordan into a huge hug. But Sara was more aware of Jase stopping what he was doing to pay attention to Amy, who wanted to show him the drawing right away.

His arm went around her, his head bent toward hers as she explained, "That's me…and you…and Mommy… and balloons."

Marissa kissed Jordan, then set him on her office chair, giving him a little ride around the area. "So, did you see the comments on the article?" she asked. "I didn't call you, because they were all good. Except for that one snide one… about how everybody should have a Raintree Winery to recover from trauma."

Sara had glanced at the comments online over her lunch break and again before she'd left work. Marissa was right. They'd all been positive. Her interview as well as Ann Custer's, the army wife whose husband was serving in Afghanistan, had been the subject of conversation among patients today, too. They'd mentioned they'd never heard of The Mommy Club before Jase's article and they were glad he was publicizing the organization.

But Sara had had other things on her mind. She said to Marissa, "I'm glad you and Liam talked me into letting Jase put my story into print. Maybe other parents who have been helped will come forward, too."

"Jase got a call from Cal. A newspaper in Sacramento wants to carry the series. Jase is going to become famous again." She saw the look on Sara's face. "Is that good or bad?"

"He could leave again," Sara said lightly.

"And you don't want that."

"No, I don't. But I'm not sure what I want matters." She wasn't saying what she was really thinking—that she wasn't sure if *she* mattered. Sex was one thing and love was another. She did love Jase, but she wasn't sure that love was returned.

"I'd better corral Amy," she said.

Marissa's expression was sympathetic, as if she understood it all. Maybe she did. Hadn't she been involved with a cowboy who'd left?

Jase was still listening to Amy's chatter as Sara approached him. When his gaze met hers, she felt all trembly again, as she had in the garage after they'd made love. What on earth had she been thinking? Obviously she hadn't been thinking or she never would have had sex with him without protection. What if she *did* get pregnant?

She'd deal with it. Just as she'd dealt with everything else that had come along. A baby was a precious gift and Jase's baby—

Well, she'd let him play whatever part he wanted to in his child's life. What else was there to do when she loved him?

"Good response to the article," he said. "I've even had more volunteers for interviews."

"I'm going to push Jordan," Amy announced, seeing what fun the little boy was having as Marissa pushed him on the rolling chair around the office.

"She and Jordan make a great pair," Jase said, and then he pointed to the drawing Amy had left on his desk. "I guess that's the three of us at the festival."

"Children remember the good times," Sara said.

"I thought you might call to tell me what Kiplinger had to say."

"I called him this morning and left a message. He didn't call me back until this afternoon. All he would say was that he'd give me High Point's decision on Friday."

"Are you sure you don't want me to postpone my trip to San Diego?"

"I'm sure. Whatever the decision is, the ramifications will still be here when you get back."

Seeing Marissa was occupied, Jase took Sara's hand and pulled her toward him for a kiss. But she stopped him. "Someone could walk in."

He canvassed her face for a long moment. "Yes, they could. At some point you're going to have to decide whether we're a couple...or not." He didn't step back; rather he held her even closer. "I have a dinner meeting in town, but I can come by tonight."

And what would happen tonight? Was she ready to admit to Jase what she felt for him? Would she invite him into her bedroom and make the decision that she was having this affair no matter whether Jase stayed at Raintree or resurrected his career?

An hour later, Sara was still thinking about Jase and his photojournalistic talent as she readied a supper of toasted turkey and cheese sandwiches, fresh fruit and raw baby carrots. Amy liked all of the above. Maybe afterward, she and Amy would bake some of those chocolate chip cookies Jase liked so much. For now, her daughter was in her room, drawing another picture and plastering it with butterfly and cat stickers.

When someone knocked on the door, Sara couldn't imagine who it might be...unless maybe Kaitlyn had stopped by for a visit after reading the interview.

But it wasn't Kaitlyn. When she answered the door, she found Liam, and he was carrying a bouquet of mixed flowers.

"This is a surprise!" Then she remembered her manners. "Come on in."

He handed her the flowers. "You did a great job with the interview. The flowers are for your guts in doing it."

"Jase's writing kept it from being maudlin or overly dramatic or too sensational. I just told what happened."

"You made it real…the way you felt when you realized the house was on fire, escaping with Amy, moving in here and having to accept help. That photo of you and Amy was great. It was really touching, Sara. I mean it."

Liam didn't look quite like himself and Sara wasn't sure why.

"I'm going to put these in water." The daisies, mums and tulips really were lovely. She took a tall glass from the cupboard, filled it with water, then quickly arranged the flowers and set it on the counter.

"I had another reason for stopping by," he said almost sheepishly. "Are you busy right now? I mean, can you take a few moments from Amy?"

Unsure of what Liam had in mind, Sara arched her brow. "To do what?"

"I was rock climbing yesterday," he said with a resigned sigh.

She studied him again more closely. His one shoulder looked to be lower than the other as if there were tension in it, as if he was in pain. "What did you do?"

"I don't know what I did. That's just it. People tell me I'm getting too old for rock climbing and I really don't want to listen. So don't give me *that* lecture." There was something about Liam that she liked…not in a man-woman way, but in a bantering-friend kind of way. "I don't give lectures."

"That's good because I don't need one. I want you to look at my shoulder."

"Liam, I'm not a doctor."

"That's the whole point. I want to know if I have to *see* a doctor. I really don't want to go through the whole emergency room routine—hours waiting, X-rays. I thought if you could just look at it, tell me what you think I did—"

She wasn't a doctor, but she did treat patients every day. However, no matter what she found, she'd tell him he needed to see a physician. The question was—could it wait or did he need to see one right now?

"Amy is coloring and plastering stickers all over the page. That will take her a while. So I have a few minutes."

"Do you need me to take my shirt off?"

"If you want me to look at your shoulder, I do."

Liam was wearing a snap-button shirt, probably easier to get into than an over-the-head T. Remembering what he'd told her, she asked, "So if you go rock climbing once a month, how do you keep in shape for it?"

"I work out three times a week to keep my muscles strengthened."

"Even so, they lose their elasticity over time. It's tough getting older, but it happens to all of us."

"Yeah, like you have to worry about it anytime soon." He shook his head. "Women worry about wrinkles. Men worry about not being able to do push-ups."

She laughed until she studied the way he was holding his arm after he took his shirt off. "What exactly did you do?"

"I wrenched it when I fell."

"I hope not far."

"About six feet. I rolled but I landed on it."

She could easily see that Liam did keep himself in shape. She studied him as she would any patient. "Does your neck hurt?"

"No. Just my shoulder."

"Turn around and let me try to figure out what you've injured."

* * *

When Jase's dinner appointment was canceled, he found himself smiling. He could spend the evening with Sara… and Amy. After Amy went to bed, they could talk more about what happened in the garage…what would happen if she became pregnant…what would happen if they became a couple. Last night he'd actually started envisioning the three of them living here in the main house. After Friday, she'd have answers and she could start planning her life all over again.

Jase liked the feeling of adrenaline that rushed through him when he walked toward Sara's cottage. He enjoyed the anticipation that heated his blood. He tried to forget about everything his father had said and everything he didn't want to think about.

But the scene with his dad last night played in his head like an unwanted movie. "Why are you running off to Africa again?" his father had asked.

"I'm not running off. I'm doing what I do best."

"Yes, you won a prize. Yes, you're an accomplished photographer and journalist. But Raintree is your home. You keep running away from it as if I've done something horrible to you. Or is the vineyard somewhere you just stop over at when you don't know where else to go?"

"I never promised to stay here. I never promised to take it over someday. In fact, you never asked me if I would."

"Asked you? You're my son!"

"Am I?"

The question had hung in the air between them…all of the conversations they'd never had, his father's remoteness, the childhood he couldn't escape. When he'd arrived at Raintree, his father had kept a distance between them, and that distance had stayed all these years. It was still there now.

"You're going to do what you want to do. You always have," his father said with a bit of resentment.

Then Jase had asked the one question that had burned in his mind, that had been stinging there all these years. "After you adopted me, did you really want to keep me? Didn't you want to send me back where I'd come from?"

Ethan actually looked shocked, then dismayed, then sad. "The idea of adopting a child was different than the reality of it."

"So you *did* want to send me back."

"No, I didn't. But I also didn't know how to relate to you. I didn't know how to comfort a child who didn't want any comfort."

"Don't lay your coldness on a twelve-year-old who had no place else to go."

Jase had walked away from that conversation last night feeling as he had when he was younger—with the need to find his own place in the world.

And now he'd found Sara.

He rapped lightly before he opened the cottage's door. After he did, it took a few moments for everything he saw to register.

As it did, he took a step back.

He saw Liam, shirtless and fit. He saw Sara's hands moving over Liam's shoulder as if she was enjoying touching him. They were gazing at each other. There were flowers on the counter beside them. In that instant, the picture of Dana kissing another man flashed before Jase's eyes. Everything he'd felt when he'd seen it, when he'd realized and then heard Dana say she'd been unfaithful came roaring back—the betrayal, the resentment, the bitterness.

He remembered Liam's wink at Sara at the soiree, their easy conversation whenever they were together. He recalled Liam's hand on Sara's arm before the search for

Amy had begun, as well as Liam saying, "I'm glad to see she's taking my advice," when she was considering letting her interview go into print.

A sense of betrayal hit Jase again—even sharper and more painful than what he'd felt with Dana. The ache he experienced now was so deep it was worse than the gunshot wounds.

Disappointment in Sara and everything they'd shared forced words out of his mouth. "I guess you really do prefer older men. I guess what happened between us doesn't matter at all."

Liam and Sara had both been focused on each other, but now they turned to him and stared at him as if he'd grown two heads.

Liam stepped forward. "Jase, you're wrong. Whatever you're thinking is wrong."

Sara took a step toward him. "Jase!"

"Wrong? I can see exactly what's going on," he said to Liam. "You don't have a shirt on. Sara's hands are on you. Two and two make four."

"And maybe you're looking through a distorted lens," Liam suggested calmly.

Now Sara seemed frozen...stricken.

Plucking his shirt off of the chair, slipping one arm into it, Liam just threw the other sleeve around his shoulder. "If you really think it's the rotator cuff," he said to Sara, "I'll drive to the E.R."

Sara had paled at Jase's words. She was practically sheet-white as she now glanced from him to Liam. "I can't tell for sure. You'll need tests, probably an MRI. I don't think you should drive yourself."

This conversation wasn't making sense to Jase, not with the flowers and the way they'd been looking at each other.

"Rotator cuff?" A foreboding began in his solar plexus and spread through his chest.

"It's probably better if Sara explains herself," Liam said, and exited the cottage.

Face-to-face with Sara, Jase asked, "What was going on?"

Her face began to take on color again as she crossed her arms over her chest. "It was obvious what you *thought* was going on. How you could even imagine I'd be attracted to Liam after what you and I—" She stopped as if embarrassed by the thought.

"You don't even want anyone to know we're seeing each other."

"Because of gossip. Because of the winery's reputation. For the sake of *my* reputation."

"Oh, Sara, is that all it is? Maybe you're not ready to start anything new."

"And you are? We began an affair and you're going to go flying off to Africa."

An affair. That *was* what he'd started, trying to tell himself they were living in the now instead of the future. Trying not to think ahead. Trying to make the most of passion he expected to end without warning.

Maybe his father had been right about him. Did he fly away from what might hurt him? Fly away from what might give him roots? But what exactly had Sara been doing with Liam?

As if she could still see his doubts, as if she could still hear the questions in his mind, as if she knew Dana was still a ghost haunting him, she explained, "Liam was rock climbing yesterday. He fell and wrenched his shoulder. He didn't want to go to the hospital and he asked me to check to see what I thought was going on with it. That's all, Jase. That's *all*."

The way she said the words alerted him to what was coming next. She was fired up and he braced himself for her words.

"Amy's in the next room coloring. Do you think I'd do anything like you were thinking with her here? Do you think I'd do anything like you were thinking when I just spent the weekend making love to *you?*"

What could he say? For just those few moments he *had* thought it.

"If you don't trust me, Jase, we don't have anything. I went through a marriage where my husband didn't trust me. He didn't trust me to tell me what was happening— that our finances were going down the tubes…that his business was failing…that our child was a burden he didn't always want."

But Sara's tone fired Jase's pride and anger, too. "Trust goes two ways. Do *you* trust *me?* Do you trust that I'll stand beside you if you're pregnant?"

"Maybe I don't want someone who's just going to stand beside me. Maybe I want more than that."

Did he even know how to give more? He never had, so he wasn't sure.

Suddenly Amy came running in from her bedroom. "Mommy. Mommy. Look."

Sara tore her gaze from his and took Amy's picture in her hand. "It's beautiful, honey."

Although Sara was trying to react normally, Jase could hear the tremble in her voice.

Amy looked up at Jase. "Are you gonna stay for supper?"

He looked at Sara and her daughter, and now he saw what he hadn't seen before—the preparations for a meal, the chocolate chips on the counter. She'd been about to make cookies for later. He didn't know what to say. He didn't know if he could repair the damage he'd done, if they could return to the passion and bliss of the weekend.

It seemed they both had a lot to think about. "Not tonight, honey. Maybe another time."

Sara didn't second that. She didn't look as if she wanted him here ever again. They'd needed space once before, and it had brought some clarity. Wasn't space what always helped him think better? Didn't space always bring him peace?

When Sara laid her hand on her daughter's head, he could see her remembering her broken marriage. He could feel her walls going up again. He could feel her closing him out of her life.

She said, "If I don't see you again before your trip Friday, have a good flight."

In other words, she needed space, too.

When he left the cottage, he didn't know why this time seeking space felt so wrong.

## Chapter Thirteen

Mr. Kiplinger wore a serious expression when he sat down with Sara in her cottage on Friday morning. She'd both dreaded and anticipated this appointment. Thinking about Jase all week had kept her from dwelling on it too much, though. She hadn't seen him and he hadn't searched her out. She didn't know what he was thinking or feeling. She realized now how the situation with Liam had looked. Maybe none of it would have happened if she'd told Jase how she felt about him.

Still, could she commit herself to a relationship that might be more long-distance than real life? Could Jase?

When Mr. Kiplinger opened his briefcase, Sara didn't know what to expect. Her original policy? A report from the investigator? A finding that she was in the wrong and they wouldn't be paying out?

Instead of a sheaf of papers or a manila envelope, Mr. Kiplinger handed her a check. "I'm sorry about the delay," he said. "The investigation showed a faulty extension cord was the cause of the fire."

"An extension cord?" she asked.

"Yes, in the laundry room."

She glanced at the check in her hand and her heart fluttered when she saw the amount. She and Amy could now get a place of their own.

Although Sara had taken a personal day today, she'd taken Amy to day care in case the meeting hadn't gone well. But it had, and now she knew there was something she must do. She had to tell Ethan Cramer she'd be leaving. He'd surely be glad to hear that.

After she thanked Mr. Kiplinger again, shook his hand and watched him drive away, Sara went to the main house to the door leading into the kitchen. She hoped Ethan was nearby. She could have phoned him, but she wanted to tell him the news face-to-face.

When Ethan answered the door, he looked awful. He was dressed in pajamas and a robe with a tissue in his hand. "You might not want to come in," he told her. "I caught some kind of bug."

His face was flushed and his eyes were a little glassy. "Do you have a fever?"

"I haven't taken my temperature," he mumbled.

"I think you should. Have you eaten yet today?"

"No, I was in bed till a few minutes ago."

"Did Jase leave?"

"Before dawn. He doesn't know I caught a cold. I wasn't going to have him postponing his trip because I started sneezing."

"Why don't you go sit in your favorite chair and I'll make you some breakfast. You need to push liquids."

"Why would you do that?" he asked brusquely. Sara

suspected that, though he was bristly on the outside, Ethan Cramer wasn't that way on the inside.

"Because you're Jase's father," she replied. "And, no, I'm not doing it so you'll let me stay in the cottage longer. The insurance company settled with me, and I'll be moving out as soon as I find a place."

"Moving out? What about you and Jase?" Ethan looked absolutely in shock.

"Mr. Cramer, I don't know if Jase wants me here any more than you do."

After a quick assessment of her, he gave a resigned sigh. "That's a bunch of nonsense. I don't know what happened between the two of you, but he's been a bear for the past week. Maybe you should think about fixing it. I'll be in the parlor. My head's pounding so hard, I can hardly stand here and talk to you."

Sara didn't know where the parlor was, but she'd find it as soon as she'd made Ethan's breakfast.

The Cramer kitchen was well stocked, and Sara easily found a frying pan, the toaster, the teapot and a hand juicer. In twenty minutes, everything was ready. She carried the tray down a hall, hearing a TV in one of the side rooms. She hadn't been in this part of the house the night of the soiree. Following the sounds, she spotted the doorway and found, indeed, she was in a parlor. There was a piano, bookshelves, a wing chair and a recliner. Ethan was in the recliner, his legs up, his head against the chair back.

His eyes flew open when he heard her enter the room. "Needed the TV louder than the pounding in my head," he explained, though he really didn't have to.

"You really should call the doctor and make an appointment. This could be more than a cold."

"Nonsense. It'll pass. I just need to break the fever."

"Hopefully breakfast will help. I made herbal tea so it doesn't dehydrate you, and if your stomach's not upset, you should drink all of the orange juice."

He switched off the television. "My stomach's fine. But I am cold."

The room was anything but cold. She picked up a throw that was spread over the back of a wing chair and handed it to him. She didn't think he would take to a lot of coddling.

He spread it over his robe. "Don't stand there holding that tray all day. The food will get cold."

Yes, it would. "Do you want the whole tray or a dish at a time?" She was already setting the tea and juice on the table beside him.

"Just add the toast to the plate with the eggs. That will be fine."

She did that and handed him the plate and a fork. "I hope you like scrambled."

"I like eggs any which way."

"Do you want me to stay while you eat or come back for the tray?"

"I don't expect either."

She smiled and sat in the wing chair. "Then I'll keep you company while you eat."

After he ate in silence for a few moments, he said, "You know, I was wrong about you."

"Because the insurance company cleared me?" This was a man who respected honesty, so she wasn't going to beat around the bush.

"No. I'd figured out before today that you wouldn't set a fire."

Curious, she asked, "How did you come to that conclusion?"

"I saw how upset you were when Amy was missing. She really is your world."

"She's everything that matters most."

"I guess it's important to tell kids how you feel…show them how you feel. You do that with your daughter. And I see Marissa doing that with Jordan, too."

"They won't know if we don't tell them and show them."

After Ethan had taken a few more bites of his scrambled eggs, he tried a piece of toast. "Feels good going down," he said. "My throat's a little scratchy."

"If you'd like soup for dinner, I can make it." With Jase away, she felt someone should care for his dad.

"You don't have to do that."

"I know I don't have to. But you've been kind to me while I've been here, letting me stay in the cottage, finding Amy."

"So this is payback?"

"Good payback, I hope. I like to feel I can help, too."

After Ethan thought about what she'd said, he nodded. "You've helped my son. You helped him when he came back from Kenya and you're helping him now."

"Any therapist could have gotten him on his feet again."

"And could any therapist teach him how to *feel* again?"

Sara kept silent because she didn't know what to say… or where this was going.

Laying down his fork, Ethan rested his head against the chair back. "I made so many mistakes with Jase I can't even count them."

As he paused, Sara kept silent. Maybe this was something Ethan needed to get off his chest. Practicing with her could help him communicate with Jase.

"When he arrived here," Jase's father went on, "I was not ready for a rebellious child. My wife and I wanted kids badly. We tried, then she died and I went into a funk. For some reason I thought the only way out of it was by forming the family she'd always wanted. So I looked into adopting. I figured I wouldn't be able to care for an infant all that easily, but an older child I could handle. That was a crock!"

"Because Jase came with a history that was hard to shake?"

"He told you?" Again Ethan seemed surprised.

"Yes, he did. I think maybe he was testing my reaction."

"That's my fault. I've always kept his background under wraps because I thought that was better for him. But he believed I was ashamed of the fact that his mother died of a drug overdose…that he was illegitimate. He thought I never considered him my real son. Even now, I'm not sure he believes I do."

"Then you have to change his mind."

"I don't know if I can. And if he flies off to Africa again, he might never come back."

"If you tell him how you feel, I don't think that will be true."

Ethan closed his eyes, then opened them again. "And what about *you?* You don't want him going to Africa, do you? Let alone Alabama or the next ten places on his list."

"I see a lot of patients in my practice, Mr. Cramer. One thing I know—none of them wants regrets. And all of them need dreams. If they know what they're good at, I encourage getting back into the swing of whatever it is. Jase wasn't just hurt physically when he was shot…and when Dana left him. He was shaken up emotionally. It took two years for him to pick up a camera again, for him to write again. That's a breakthrough in itself. As much as I don't want him to go, I know he has to. He has a gift for the pictures he takes and the stories he writes. That's part of him. If I love him, I have to accept that."

Somehow, talking about this now helped clarify in her mind and heart what she wanted…and needed. If she loved Jase, she could accept him unconditionally, no matter where his career took him. Somehow they would make their relationship work. *If* he loved her. *If* he trusted her.

Ethan jumped on her conclusion. "*Do* you love my son?"

"I do. But everything got messed up this week. We had a misunderstanding. It brought up some basic problems that we might not be able to resolve."

"If you love Jase and he loves you, of course they can be resolved. My Martha and I were strong-willed people. We disagreed a lot. Somehow we found compromise and we knew neither of us was going anywhere. At least that's what we told ourselves. Neither of us expected fate to change all that. So if you *do* love Jase, certainly there is some way to fix this misunderstanding."

Sara lowered her eyes, studied her hands. "He didn't trust me."

"Did you give him a good reason *to* trust you?"

At first she almost became angry because Jase knew her so well…knew who she was…knew what she'd been through. However, as she stopped to think about it now and what Jase had seen as he'd walked in the door, maybe, just maybe she could have prevented the whole situation. After they'd made love, if she'd told Jase she loved him, if she'd told him she wanted his baby, then maybe he would have seen the tableau with her and Liam differently. Maybe then he wouldn't have doubted.

What would happen if she told him now? Could they get back the best of what they'd felt? Would Jase trust her? Could they have a future?

Although Sara hadn't answered his question, Ethan didn't probe for an answer. "Jase didn't look too happy before he left. And I expect he'll do some thinking while he's gone. Staying in a hotel room alone gives a person lots of time to dwell on everything he doesn't want to dwell on." Ethan studied her. "When did this misunderstanding happen?"

"On Monday."

"So why haven't you and Jase talked since then?" After he asked the question, he suddenly held up his hand. "You don't have to say. You were probably mad about something and Jase— The first thing he does when he gets hurt is put distance between him and whoever hurt him. Believe me, I know that for sure."

"But if he wants the distance—"

"I didn't say he wanted it. It's just something he learned to do from the time he was a kid. My guess is that the best thing for him would be somebody helping him to change that pattern." Ethan handed Sara his plate. "You think about that while I try to drink all these liquids you brought me."

"If you'd like chicken soup, I can make it this afternoon and see that you have dinner before I pick up Amy."

"Mrs. Tiswald makes chicken soup now and then, but she doesn't put corn in it, even though I tell her I like it. Can you do that?"

"Sure, I can. Noodles or rice?"

"Noodles."

"Consider it done, Mr. Cramer."

She'd put the dishes on the tray, then reached the doorway when Ethan called her name. "Sara."

She turned.

"Call me Ethan."

As she carried the tray to the kitchen, she was smiling—genuinely smiling—for the first time all week. Maybe now that she'd made progress with Ethan, she'd make progress with his son. If she could show and tell Jase she loved him, maybe then he could trust her...maybe then they could both reach for a dream.

On the return flight to Sacramento, in the window seat, Jase thought about all of the hotel rooms he'd stayed in over the years and why the one at the hotel he'd recently vacated had been intolerable. The meetings had gone swimmingly well. He and Tony had had a dinner meeting with a new distributor who would be spreading the word about their wines at three different conventions, three different organizations of professionals who, if they liked the wine, would talk it up to their friends, colleagues and other professionals. Although Jase had tried to keep his mind on business during the past two days, that had been tough, as tough as it had been since Monday. His thoughts had wandered constantly to Sara and what had happened.

He'd been wrong. All week he'd made excuses for himself but none were good enough. Would she be able to forgive his doubts? Was he willing to give up his trip to Africa? How much *did* she mean to him?

Last night in his hotel room, turmoil had raged inside of him. All he'd remembered was another hotel room, another bed and another sleepless night. He'd felt so vulnerable. And maybe *that* was his problem.

In first-class seats, Tony sat beside him with a glass of Scotch. Jase hadn't touched his yet. He didn't confide his thoughts and feelings to many people. But Tony had become a trusted friend over the past two years. He didn't gossip. He didn't talk out of hand and he certainly didn't break confidences. So maybe he'd be a good sounding board.

After Tony downed at least half of his Scotch, he asked Jase, "What's on your mind? You've been preoccupied this whole trip."

"Don't tell me I'm that transparent."

"Not to most people. But I know you, Jase, and something's bothering you. What is it? This trip to Africa you're planning?"

He'd told Tony about that on the flight down. "No, something else is on my mind. Can I ask you some personal questions?"

Tony gave him a wry smile. "That depends on how personal."

Recognizing the landscape as the plane neared the airport, Jase asked, "Have you ever doubted your decision to get married?"

Tony's reply was instantaneous. "Never." His friend gave him a probing look. Then he added, "Connie and I might not always agree, but we're committed to each other. There's no one I'd rather be with, no one I'd rather have as my best friend, no one I feel more comfortable with and no one else who I could imagine waking up with every morning. She's it for me. Why are you asking? Thinking about getting married?"

Jase glanced out the window and noticed their plane seemed to be circling, just as the thoughts were circling in his mind. Since Dana, he hadn't thought that he was suited for marriage or that he could stay in one place. Never thought anybody would love him forever.

But Sara—

Almost immediately after he'd said the words that had ruined everything between them, he'd known he was wrong. No matter how the situation had looked, she wasn't the type of woman who lied…or cheated. She was the type of woman who would be loyal. She was the type of woman who knew how to love. Maybe if he could tell her he'd been jealous and that's why the doubts had arisen, maybe if he could tell her he wanted her for his own, maybe if he could tell her how he felt, he could convince her he could truly put the past behind him and find a future with her.

"*Are* you thinking about getting married?" Tony repeated.

"I am," Jase confirmed. "Now I just have to convince Sara that sometimes men in love make mistakes and ask her to forgive me."

Tony raised his glass in a toast. "You'll convince her."

Jase hoped his friend was right. But as he noticed their plane circling the area again, he knew he'd use the time to find just the right words to convince her he loved her.

Sara was nervous on Saturday evening, more nervous than she'd ever been. She was about to risk her heart. If Jase couldn't return her love, she'd have to accept that. But if she didn't say what she felt and she lost him, she'd have no one but herself to blame. She didn't want to have regrets.

As she set up the picnic in the Merlot vineyard under an oak's shade, she thought about Ethan. He was feeling better today and his fever had broken. Last evening, she'd taken him chicken soup for dinner with toasted bread and applesauce. He'd eaten it all. She'd checked on him again by phone before bed and he'd been dozing. She'd told him to call her if he needed her. This morning he *had* called to tell her he was making his own breakfast and he didn't want her to expose Amy to more of his germs. No, he hadn't heard from Jase but expected him home around five.

Last night she'd left a note with Ethan that he was supposed to give Jase when he returned. When she'd called Marissa, her friend had excitedly volunteered to stay with Amy and await the outcome of this picnic.

Eagerly, Sara arranged a yellow checkered tablecloth with festive paper plates and napkins…and even a vase of wildflowers in the center of the cloth. The cooler was filled with fried chicken, potato salad, fresh strawberries and cheese. A bottle of her favorite Raintree wine was chilled. She just needed Jase.

But five o'clock passed. Six o'clock came and went. Had he gotten the note? Or was he going to ignore her invitation?

She was about ready to give up, to fold up her dreams and pack them back into her heart, but then she saw him walking toward her. The wind tossed his hair, but as he got closer, his shadow fell across the tablecloth and she saw his expression was somber. Was he late because he couldn't make up his mind whether he should come or not? Was he late because he was going to tell her they were finished? The answer to either of those made her sad to the depths of her soul.

"I didn't think you were going to come," she blurted out honestly.

"My plane landed late. We had to circle because another plane had difficulty on the runway and air traffic had to be rerouted."

She was so relieved her knees felt weak, but a hurdle still lay before her. "So you'll stay and have a picnic with me? I…I made something for you."

"Sara, I have something to tell you."

She was afraid to hear it. But she handed him a scrapbook. "Look at this first, okay?"

When he hesitated, all of her fears reared up again. But then Jase sank to the ground cross-legged, and that gave her hope. He started paging through the scrapbook. It was filled with the photos he'd given her of the three of them—pictures of the day he'd used his camera again when they'd aimed the hose at each other and he and Amy had hopscotched. He had snapped more photos the day of the festival, setting the timer, catching Amy with her balloon and the two of them eating pastries. He'd caught Amy chasing a butterfly, Sara walking through the vineyard, both her and Amy sitting at the picnic table as he'd grilled burgers.

Before she lost her chance, she said, "I want these pictures to be more than memories. My settlement came through, and I can leave now if you want me to."

What came next was the tough part, the laying-her-heart-on-the-line part. "But I love you, Jase Cramer. And I'd like to be in your life permanently." She hurried on. "If you want to photograph children at a clinic in Africa, I'll support you in that. I understand your gifts and your need to use them. I guess I just want you to know I'll always be here waiting for you."

Jase put the album aside and took both of her hands in his. "I've done a lot of soul-searching since Monday. I'm so sorry I jumped to the wrong conclusion. I think we both know why. Once before, you helped me believe in a new life and now I'm believing in one again...one where you and Amy and I can be a real family...where I can be the husband and dad I never thought I could be. I promise I will learn how to do both."

"You don't have much to learn," she said, stroking his

stubbornly defined jaw, her being overflowing with so much happiness it filled up the world.

"Can you forgive what I thought?" he asked in a husky voice.

"I've been putting myself in your shoes, seeing what you thought you saw. I probably would have reacted the same way. We want to belong to each other, Jase, and I love the idea of that."

"And I love you," he said with so much love she felt it through to her heart and soul. "Will you marry me?"

"Yes, I'll marry you." She wanted to make a life with him and be with him no matter where that led her.

Jase took her in his arms and kissed her.

## *Epilogue*

Jase had overseen many weddings at the vineyard, but this one was going to top them all. As he stood before a flowered trellis, he marveled at the way Marissa had transformed the gardens. They were alive with the colors of late August, and she'd added canopies and white chairs. A trio of musicians played a harp, guitar and cello. Most of all, she'd listened to his wishes as well as Sara's, putting framed photographs of the three of them on every table, adding disposable cameras so the guests could take photographs that were candid and expressive. Sure, they'd hired the usual photographer and videographer, but Jase had wanted their friends' takes on what they saw and the happiness they felt. Because everyone did seem happy... even his dad.

Since he and Sara had gotten engaged, his relationship with his dad had changed. Maybe it had started when she'd moved into the cottage. But now Jase understood his father better and wasn't as quick to take offense. Ethan was easily accepting Sara as his daughter and Amy as his granddaughter with an enthusiasm that Jase hadn't seen in a long time. They'd all spent the past six weeks planning, compromising, making decisions.

Beside Jase now, Tony said, "So you're not going to Africa?"

"Not this time. I *am* going to Alabama, though. And Sara and Amy are coming with me. That trip will be about kids and schools and getting the word out for donations to help build a library."

His best man probed a little deeper. "So you're going to live in Raintree's main house?"

He nodded. "We're going to remodel first. Dad's all for it. He'd like a suite of rooms on the first floor. He said that makes sense as he gets older. We'll do some remodeling upstairs, too, for us. After our honeymoon in Aruba, Sara and Amy and I will stay at the cottage while all of that is going on. Dad's going to take a trip to France with Liam and visit some wineries. He's wanted to do it for a while but didn't feel free to leave the vineyard."

"But now he does."

"He does. He knows I think of it as home now. I might take a jaunt every once in a while to fulfill journalistic tendencies, but I'm going to remain general manager... and take over someday."

The music changed in tone and everyone knew what that meant. All of the guests stood. Connie and other Mommy Club volunteers filled the first few rows. Liam was there, too, with a grin on his face as he gave Jase a thumbs-up sign.

Marissa came down the white runner first, her smile wide as she caught his eye and winked. When she reached the first row of chairs, she turned around and beckoned to the next in line. Amy and Jordan walked up the aisle hand in hand. Amy was carrying a basket of rose petals and Jordan dipped his hand into it, flinging them around every few steps. When they reached the front, Marissa gathered the kids and settled them into chairs next to her on the right. Kaitlyn came next and then—

Then there was Sara on his father's arm.

She looked like a princess…or Cinderella. The gown was mounds of tulle with seed pearls, embroidery and glass beads. It was strapless. The tulle veil covered her shoulders and draped down the back. She was almost too beautiful to look at, but Jase looked anyway. He'd be looking at her like this forever.

When Sara met him at the trellis, she gave his dad a kiss on the cheek. His father was still a bit red-faced as he shook Jase's hand and said, "Congratulations, son."

Jase's throat tightened. For the first time since he'd arrived at Raintree, they had a true father-son bond.

After his dad took his seat beside Marissa, Jase bent close to Sara and murmured, "You're the most beautiful bride I've ever seen. I love you."

Her eyes glistened with happiness as she said the words, too. "I love *you*. I'm so happy I'm going to burst."

"Not yet," he teased. "Remember we have a celebration after the wedding."

In unison they turned toward the minister, standing close, holding each other's hands.

After the minister welcomed everyone and said an opening prayer, Jase and Sara faced each other for their vows.

Jase went first. "I, Jase Cramer, take you, Sara Stevens, to be my wife. I promise to love you, cherish you and Amy, honor you and be faithful to you. My commitment to you isn't just for today. It's for the rest of our lives…and beyond. It will grow deeper each day as I become the husband you need and the father Amy deserves. I will learn to put our family first and my desires second. We've already begun the art of compromise and I look forward to more of it. I vow to give you all I can and everything I am. I love you, Sara Stevens, and I am proud to become your husband today."

Sara's tears showed him how much his promises meant to her. They hadn't heard each other's vows because they hadn't wanted them to be practiced. They'd wanted the words to come from their hearts.

After Sara squeezed his fingers, she said, "I love you, Jase Cramer, more than I ever thought I could love. And still I look forward to that love growing each and every day as we make a new life together. I promise to honor you, cherish you, respect you and listen to you. With all my heart I want you to be Amy's real dad. And I promise to trust you with her and with any decisions we make about her. No matter where we live, I will make us a home where we will feel free to say our minds, feel free to express our concerns, feel free to love. We've both searched for someone to belong to for a long time. I know we belong together. Our dreams for our lives and Amy's are within our grasp. I promise you my heart, Jase...and that I will take good care of yours. I love you, and I can't wait to be your wife."

They squeezed each other's hands and Jase knew he'd always remember this moment. The minister said a few more words, and then Jase and Sara exchanged rings. He'd bought her a diamond big enough to catch abundant sunlight every day. But for a wedding ring she'd asked for a plain gold band and that's what he would wear, too.

Jase and Sara had asked the minister to do something a little different. Before the blessing, they brought Amy up with them. Jase held her in one arm with his other arm around Sara as the minister said, "I now pronounce you husband and wife. I pronounce you a family."

Jase set Amy on the ground. She ran to Jordan and Marissa, and he took Sara in his arms again and kissed her.

The guests applauded and Marissa whistled. Tony congratulated them both.

Then Sara reached her hand out to Amy once more and the three of them walked down the white runner to the beginning of a new life.

\* \* \* \* \*

*Look for Adam & Kaitlyn's story,*
*the next book in Karen Rose Smith's new miniseries,*
THE MOMMY CLUB.
*Coming soon to Harlequin Special Edition!*

**COMING NEXT MONTH**
**from Harlequin® Special Edition®**
AVAILABLE AUGUST 20, 2013

## #2281 THE MAVERICK & THE MANHATTANITE
*Montana Mavericks: Rust Creek Cowboys*
**Leanne Banks**
When Sheriff Gage Christensen meets energetic Lissa Roarke, a volunteer helping with Rust Creek's flood restoration efforts, he soon finds he's got more than rebuilding the town on his mind.

## #2282 THE ONE WHO CHANGED EVERYTHING
*The Cherry Sisters*
**Lilian Darcy**
Daisy Cherry annoys her sister Lee when she hires Lee's ex-fiancé, Tucker, for a landscaping project. Little does Daisy know there's more than old enmity brewing between her and Tucker....

## #2283 A VERY SPECIAL DELIVERY
*Those Engaging Garretts!*
**Brenda Harlen**
Lukas Garrett miraculously delivers Julie Marlowe's son during a blizzard. Though Lukas bonds with Julie and newborn, Caden, can the couple overcome Julie's tragic past to create a bright new future?

## #2284 LOST AND FOUND FATHER
*Family Renewal*
**Sheri WhiteFeather**
In high school, Ryan Nash abandoned his pregnant girlfriend, Victoria. When Victoria contacts her now-adult daughter and takes her to meet Ryan, sparks fly—and a family is born.

## #2285 THE BONUS MOM
**Jennifer Greene**
While on a hike, botanist Rosemary MacKinnon finds more than she bargained for—handsome widower Whit and his twin daughters. The outdoorsy duo forms a bond, but can family spring anew from emotional ashes?

## #2286 DOCTOR, SOLDIER, DADDY
*The Doctors MacDowell*
**Caro Carson**
When army doc Jamie MacDowell marries orderly Kendry Harrison, he just wants a mother for his newborn son. But can he overcome his past to recognize love in the present?

You can find more information on upcoming Harlequin® titles, free excerpts and more at www.Harlequin.com.

HSECNM0813

SPECIAL EXCERPT FROM

◆ **HARLEQUIN**®
™

# SPECIAL EDITION

*When city girl Lissa Roarke comes to
Rust Creek Falls to assist with the cleanup efforts after
the Great Montana Flood, she butts heads with
Sheriff Gage Christensen. He doesn't trust outsiders,
and seems bent on making Lissa's life miserable.
Little does he know that she's the cure for what ails him....*

\*\*\*

"**I**'m so excited I can't stand it," she admitted. "We can finally start getting something done."

Her enthusiasm burrowed inside him. He smiled. "Yeah, that's good. And we all appreciate it."

"Thanks," she said. "I'm going to make an early night of it, so I'll be ready to greet the volunteers tomorrow. Thank you for getting me some wheels."

"My pleasure," Gage said. "But no—"

"Driving in the snow," she finished for him. "That ditch was no fun for me, either."

"It's dark. You want me to walk you back to the rooming house?" He offered because he wanted to extend his time with her.

"I think I'll be okay," she said. "Rust Creek isn't the most crime-ridden place in the world. But thank you for your chivalry."

Gage gave a rough chuckle. "No one's ever accused me of being chivalrous."

"Well, maybe they haven't been watching closely enough."

Gage felt his gut take a hard dip at her statement. He knew

that Lissa was struggling with her visit to Rust Creek and he hadn't made it as easy for her as he should have. There was some kind of electricity or something between them that he couldn't quite name. Just looking at her did something to him.

"I'll take that as a compliment. Call me if you need me," he said.

"Thank you," she said. "Good night."

"Good night," he said, and wished she was going home with him to his temporary trailer to keep him warm. Crazy, he told himself. All wrong. She was Manhattan. He was Montana. Big difference. The twain would never meet. Right?

\*\*\*

*We hope you enjoyed this sneak peek from*
**USA TODAY** *bestselling author Leanne Banks's new*
*Harlequin Special Edition book,*
**THE MAVERICK & THE MANHATTANITE,**
*the next installment in*
**MONTANA MAVERICKS: RUST CREEK COWBOYS,**
*the brand-new six-book continuity launched in July 2013!*

# SADDLE UP AND READ 'EM!

**Looking for another great Western read? Check out these September reads from HOME & FAMILY category!**

CALLAHAN COWBOY TRIPLETS by Tina Leonard
*Callahan Cowboys*
Harlequin American Romance

HAVING THE COWBOY'S BABY by Trish Milburn
*Blue Falls, Texas*
Harlequin American Romance

HOME TO WYOMING by Rebecca Winters
*Daddy Dude Ranch*
Harlequin American Romance

*Look for these great Western reads and more available wherever books are sold or visit*
**www.Harlequin.com/Westerns**